"Sweet, sweet temptress . . .

"I ache for you," he murmured, brushing his mouth against the soft bared skin of her breast. "I've wanted to do this since that first night in your kitchen. I wondered what you would taste like." His breath was hot and moist on her yearning flesh.

Pleasure seared through her. Pleasure at his words and actions. "Did you?" she asked hesitantly.

"Oh, I did. I do. And now I'm going to find out." His lips opened over her.

Lily sighed, the sound turning into a moan of feminine need. He lifted his head to look at her, and his eyes were nearly black with ardour. "Too much?" he asked softly. "Not enough?"

"Yes," she replied, answering both impossible questions. "Yes."

To all my friends in Bend,
who made my stay there so enjoyable.

———— 🍎 ————

CANDACE SCHULER
is also the author
of these novels in
Temptation

DESIRE'S CHILD
DESIGNING WOMAN
FOR THE LOVE OF MIKE

Home Fires

CANDACE SCHULER

MILLS & BOON LIMITED
ETON HOUSE, 18–24 PARADISE ROAD
RICHMOND, SURREY TW9 1SR

First published in Great Britain in 1988 by
Mills & Boon Limited, Eton House, 18–24 Paradise Road,
Richmond, Surrey. TW9 1SR

© Candace Schuler 1987

ISBN 0 263 76269 6

21-XP8811

Made and printed in Great Britain

1

LILY TALBOT struggled up from the depths of sleep, groggily trying to identify the sound that had penetrated the fog of dreams drifting around inside her head. It wasn't the storm itself that had awakened her; the rain and wind had been whipping around since late that afternoon, and she was inured to the sound. Besides, it usually took more than the flash of lightning and the clap of thunder to pry her eyes open once they had closed for the night.

Maybe one of the kids has gotten up, she thought, levering herself up on one elbow to listen more closely. None of her three were afraid of storms but Jeff had suffered from those awful nightmares right after the divorce. Maybe the storm had somehow triggered another one.

The sound came again. A muffled pounding. An almost rhythmic banging. *Not the kids*, Lily thought, sighing with relief when she realized the noise was coming from the opposite end of the lodge to the kids' bedrooms.

What was it, then?

It came again, sounding even more furious, as if the wild storm was whipping whatever it was to an even greater frenzy. A shutter? No, she reminded herself, her handyman, Tim, had secured those for the coming winter over a month ago. The screen door flailing about in the wind? No, not that, either, because she distinctly remembered latching it before going to bed. Lily sat up, her head cocked as she strained to identify the sound. It was the front door, she realized at last. Someone was pounding on the front door of the lodge.

She sat quietly for a second more, fighting the urge to just lie down and go back to sleep. It was so late, and it was so warm and cozy here in her bed, and she was so sleepy. Too sleepy to get up and deal with anyone right then, even a paying customer.

But it was a wicked night out, she thought, squinting sleepily as a blinding flash of lightning heralded another deafening clap of thunder. Unfit, as the saying went, for man or beast. And she *was* running a motel of sorts. It was probably her legal duty as the proprietor of said establishment to let the poor, rain-soaked wayfarer in and offer him—or her—shelter for the night.

And besides, it didn't sound as if her potential guest intended to go away. The furious pounding showed no signs of stopping in the near future. It seemed, in fact, to have gotten louder. Rising in volume with the storm, it rattled the windowpanes in the door and threatened to wake the children if it went on much longer. And they had to be up early for school tomorrow.

With a huge yawn, Lily pushed the covers back and groped for her blue chenille robe. Shoving her arms into the sleeves, she knotted the sash at her slender waist and hurried toward the front door of the Talbot Family Resort. Her bare toes curled against the cold wooden floor as she exited her bedroom and entered the dark lobby. Silently she made her way across the room, squinting as she tried to make out the form on the other side of the door.

The soft yellow glow of the porch light provided the only source of steady illumination between the flashes of lightning that slashed through the dark, turbulent night. It was behind the stranger, backlighting him as he stood under the overhang on the porch and pounded on the door.

Lily paused uncertainly in the middle of the dark room, feeling a faint stirring of apprehension. He was huge, his hulking shadowed image filling up the whole of the glass panes on the top half of the door. The pounding suddenly sounded almost menacing. Angry somehow, as if she had made him furious by taking so long to answer his summons.

She hesitated another moment, fully aware of just how vulnerable she really was. A divorced woman alone with three children. The only man around the place, her handyman, Tim Wade, lived out in one of the tiny cabins behind the main building. He wouldn't hear her if she screamed, not on a wild night like this.

Oh, stop being so melodramatic, Lily chided herself then, as if she were talking to one of her children. *There's no reason on earth for you to scream. He's just a weary traveler,* she told herself firmly, *looking for a dry place to spend this cold, wet, miserable night.* Squaring her shoulders, she started toward the door again, her bare feet soundless on the floor.

The pounding stopped abruptly, and the man outside cupped his hands against the glass and leaned forward to peer in the window as if he had heard her move. It made his shadow even larger, even more menacing. Lily stopped and shrank back, one hand clutching her robe to her chest as if he could actually see into the darkened room. He dropped one hand and rattled the doorknob, testing it. Lily sucked in her breath and held it.

Legal duty or not, she thought then, bad weather or not, she would just stand here—very, very quietly—until he went away. There were plenty of other motels and campgrounds in Bend. Let him go pound on someone else's door.

Her unwelcome visitor stood there for a few seconds longer, his nose pressed against the glass as he peered into the window, and then he shrugged those huge shoulders and turned away. He was caught in profile for a few moments, the feeble glow of the porch light finally illuminating his face instead of hiding it. It was a nice face, Lily thought as she stood there with her hand clutching the front of her robe and the cold from the floor slowly creeping up her legs.

He still looked big, with those shoulders that were the size of a house, but not nearly as menacing now that she could see him more clearly. His mouth was turned down in a rueful grimace as he looked out into the sleeting rain. His cheeks were lean, almost gaunt, his chin was firm, his nose fine and straight. And his jaw, although uncompromisingly hard and shadowed with a day's growth of beard, curved upward in a surprisingly vulnerable line just beneath his ear.

He looked tired, too. Bone tired. And soggy. She could see the separate, sparkling drops of water clinging to his curling rain-dark hair, running in icy little rivulets into the turned-up collar of his heavy down jacket. He shivered, hunching into the collar a little as he prepared to step off the porch into the storm. Lily's tender, maternal heart melted.

The poor man was tired and soggy and cold. Probably hungry, too, if he'd driven as long and as far as it appeared he had. Hardly the stuff desperadoes are made of.

Without another thought for her guest's possible proclivity for murder and mayhem, Lily hurried the rest of the way across the room and pulled open the front door of the lodge.

"I'm sorry I took so long to answer," she said, flicking on the interior light as she spoke. "I was sound asleep and didn't hear you at first."

The sound of her voice caught him in midmotion, just as he lifted his foot to step off the porch. He whirled around with an awkward twist of his big body, lost his balance and came stumbling toward the open door. Blinded by the glare of bright light, he reached out, groping for a handhold. Lily caught him, the palms of her hands thudding against his chest just as his booted foot came down on the tops of her bare toes. She squealed, her hands automatically gripping the bulky fabric of his jacket in reaction to the pain.

"Geez, I'm sorry, lady." His voice was rough and raspy with fatigue, laced with irritation at his clumsiness. "I didn't mean to throw myself at you like that."

He straightened away from her, pushing himself upright with a hand against the doorjamb, but Lily's fingers didn't loosen on his jacket. She seemed to be clinging to him for dear life.

"Are you all right?" He clasped her shoulders supportively, his one thought that she was holding on to him because she had to. "Did I break your toes?"

"No . . . no, I don't think so," Lily said breathlessly, her eyes closing as she tried to assess the damage by feel alone. Everything seemed to be okay, but if there was blood she didn't want to see it. "You didn't really step on them. You just, ah, grazed them a little."

He squinted against the light, trying to see her more clearly. "You're sure they're not broken?" His hands were under her elbows now, holding her up in case she felt faint.

"I don't know."

"Can you wiggle your toes?"

"I haven't tried." And she didn't want to; she might hear the crackle of broken bones. The mere thought made her want to lie down with a cold cloth over her forehead.

"Wiggle your toes," he commanded.

Lily forced herself to wiggle her toes. There was no pain except the sharp sting of grazed skin. "No, they're not broken," she said, opening her eyes at last. "They're just . . ." Her voice trailed off as she met his eyes.

They were brown. Simple brown eyes, made inexplicably fascinating by the reckless sparkle lurking just behind the concern in his expression. There was danger in their depths, too, despite the fine lines of fatigue etched at their corners, and laughter and passion and, other things Lily hadn't thought about in years. She stared into them for a helpless second or two, mesmerized by what she saw.

"Are you sure you're all right?" His hands tightened on her elbows, his brows drawing together in a frown as she continued to stare up at him. "You're not going to faint, are you?" His tone left absolutely no doubt as to his feelings about fainting women.

"No . . . no, I'm fine. Really." With an effort Lily lowered her eyes from his until they were on a level with his throat. It was strong and darkly tanned, unprotected from the cold and wet. She could see the open collar of the red-and-black flannel shirt that he wore under his down jacket and the narrow wedge of a thin waffle-weave thermal T-shirt under that. He smelled of wood smoke and musk and warm, virile man. Of their own volition her eyes moved lower. Faded snug-fitting jeans molded his lower body, faithfully delineating the male shape of him and conforming to the hard muscles of his long legs. Lily shivered slightly and forced her eyes farther down, past the temptations his body seemed to offer her. He was wearing a high-top leather hiking boot on one foot. The other was encased in a battered, rain-splattered cast.

When she saw the cast, everything that was maternal in Lily rushed to the fore, overwhelming the more

basic female emotions that had barely begun to surface. She might be a coward about her own injuries and
pain, but someone else's always brought out the mother
in her.

"What in heaven's name are you doing out on a night
like this in your condition? Don't you know that a cast
is supposed to be kept dry?" The words were scolding
and sharp, an unconscious reaction to the unaccustomed feelings that had shivered through her just seconds before. "No wonder you're stumbling all over the
place like a drunken lumberjack." One hand slid from
his chest to wrap around his waist. The other guided his
arm over her head. She wedged her shoulder under his.
"Come inside," she ordered, steering him through the
open door with the care of a nurse guiding a recently ill
patient down the corridor of a hospital. Her own
bruised toes were completely forgotten. "It's freezing
out here."

She stopped just inside the threshold, reaching back
with the hand around his waist to shut the door behind
them. "Let's just get you into the kitchen where it's
warm and I'll get you a couple of towels to dry off with,"
she said, maneuvering him around the bulky furniture
in the large main room of the lodge. "We can worry
about getting you checked in later, after you've had
something to warm you up." She patted his waist com-
fortingly. "I'll bet you'd like a cup of hot coffee,
wouldn't you? And maybe a bite to eat?"

"That I would," he agreed absently, his mind fully
occupied by the fact that the fingers of his left hand were
resting against the gentle slope of her breast. He didn't

really need her help; he was perfectly capable of walking on his own, despite the cast, but she was woman-soft under the nubby material of her robe and her small, bed-warmed body was surprisingly lush against his.

He could see a tempting wedge of white lace between the crossed lapels of her robe, threaded with a feminine bit of pink satin ribbon. Her hair was blond and beguilingly tousled, soft tendrils of it clinging to the sleeve of his jacket. She smelled of something sweet.

A real gentleman would probably move his hand, he thought. But then, when was the last time anyone had ever accused him of being a real gentleman? A small grin tugged at the corners of his mouth. It wasn't his fault that his hand was there, anyway. She was holding it in place, her slender ringless fingers wrapped firmly around his wrist as she helped him into the kitchen. He might as well enjoy it while it lasted.

He sent a silent message to his editor, mentally apologizing for all the nasty things he'd said about the man's ethics and parentage when Neil had told him what his next story assignment was—a nice easy travel-and-recreation piece to ease the invalid back to full-time work instead of covering that cross-country dogsled race in Alaska. In the ensuing battle of wills, he'd argued that researching the recreational facilities of Bend, Oregon, would be a dead bore and no challenge at all for a man of his particular skills. Now, looking down at the intriguing hint of cleavage revealed to him by his position, he revised his opinion just a little. His current assignment might not be quite as boring as he'd first thought.

He wondered if Neil had known that this cuddly little armful was the proprietor of the lodge when he'd made the reservations, if he'd meant her as a sort of a consolation prize for not giving his "favorite writer and best friend" the Alaskan story. A grin tugged at his mouth again. It was the kind of perverted thing Neil would think of—and if he weren't so damned tired he just might be tempted to find out how much of a consolation she was willing to be.

"Here we go." Lily slipped out from under his shoulder, easing him into a chair at the kitchen table. "Let's just get you out of this wet jacket," she said, reaching to push it off his shoulders with both hands. "Lean forward a little bit," she ordered, tugging first one sleeve and then the other down his arms. He felt like a little boy being undressed by his mother. "There, that's better, isn't it?"

He nodded, his eyes on the soft lift and sway of her breasts under the blue material of her robe.

"Now you just sit right there. I'll go pop this jacket in the dryer for a few minutes and bring you a towel." She disappeared into a room off the kitchen, automatically closing the door behind her so that the heat wouldn't escape.

Her guest sat where he was ordered, his tired body soaking up the warmth of the kitchen, his agile mind weaving idle fantasies about his hostess, his restless writer's eye absently taking stock of his surroundings.

The kitchen was a large room, made cozy with pale yellow walls, old-fashioned oak cabinets and checked gingham curtains at the window over the sink. There was a hooked oval rug covering the planked floor under the trestle-style table where he sat, a six-burner industrial-size stove, and what looked like dozens of miniature loaves of bread cooling on almost every available inch of counter space. They smelled almost as good as his hostess did. His mouth began to water, fantasies of the woman in the blue robe being replaced by thoughts of warm, butter-smeared bread. It had been hours since his last meal—if you could call bad coffee, greasy french fries and two bites of an overcooked hamburger a meal.

Just as he was thinking about getting up to help himself to the bread, Lily bustled back into the room with a large towel in one hand. She draped it over his head. "You shouldn't sit around with wet hair any longer than you absolutely have to," she said, rubbing briskly. "You could catch your death of cold that way."

There was a sputtering noise from under the towel.

"No, really," Lily said. "It's true. Having a wet head reduces your resistance to cold germs, especially when you're tired on top of it. And you *are* tired, even if you don't realize it," she added, thinking of how Elizabeth, her baby at six, still fought sleep to the death, as if she were afraid she would miss something if she closed her eyes. Men, she reflected for the millionth time, were a lot like kids in some ways. "Breaking that leg probably took a lot out of you, too, resistance-wise."

There was another strangled sound from under the towel.

Lily's hands paused in their task. "I'm sorry. What did you say?"

"I think I can handle it from here," he repeated, reaching up to push the towel out of his face. His eyes were on a level with the ribbon-trimmed lace of her nightgown. Another inch, he thought, and his nose would be buried between her breasts. And nice breasts they were—soft and round and sweet smelling. Despite his tiredness, he felt his body stir. "Then again—" he peered up at her from under the towel, his brown eyes alight with a teasing invitation "—maybe I can't handle it . . . alone."

Lily stared back at him for the space of a heartbeat, her brows pulled together in a puzzled little frown, her hands still holding his head. It had been a long time since a man had looked at her with that particular light in his eyes; she needed a moment to see it for what it was. A totally unexpected rush of heat surged through her, and then she gasped, snatching her hands away as if his hair were on fire.

"I'll make that coffee now." She whirled away, presenting him with her back as she yanked open a cabinet and began frantically rummaging through its contents.

What in the world is the matter with you, she chided herself. *Treating a grown man like one of the kids! Toweling him off as if he were no more than ten! Oh, Lord, what must he be thinking?*

Her cheeks reddened.

If that look he'd given her was anything to go by, she knew what he was thinking. And she couldn't let him think that because . . . because she hadn't meant anything of the kind! But she couldn't come out and say he had misunderstood her, could she? No, that would only make things worse. "The lady doth protest too much" and all that. It would be best, she decided, to just pretend it hadn't happened. Besides, nothing *had* happened. Nothing except that flash of heat passing from his eyes to hers.

"Would you like..." Lily cleared her throat and tried again. She was still facing the open cabinet. "Would you like regular coffee or decaf, Mr., ah . . ."

Oh, Lord! She didn't even know the man's name. Somehow, it made it worse to realize she'd been treating a total stranger like one of her brood. That she'd felt that moment of . . . of something for a man she didn't know from Adam. With a resigned sigh, she turned from the cabinet to face him. She hoped her cheeks weren't as red as they felt.

"I'm sorry, in all the, ah, confusion I guess we forgot to introduce ourselves. I'm Lily Talbot," she said with as much dignity as she could muster, "the owner and manager of the Talbot Family Resort."

"Saxon." He was dabbing his damp hair with the towel, his head bent as he ruffled the curls at his nape. "Grant Saxon." He flashed her a quick, boyish smile. "And I prefer regular, please."

Lily's face lit up with relief and recognition. He wasn't going to pursue the matter—and he wasn't quite a total stranger, after all. "Oh! You're Neil Baxter's writer friend. The one who needs to take it easy for a few days."

Grant stopped rubbing his hair. So Neil did know she was up here. Interesting. "How do you know Neil?"

"Oh—" she shrugged "—Neil's a regular guest at the lodge. He and his, um, friend come up here every year to go fishing."

Grant's eyes crinkled in amusement at her slight hesitation. Knowing Neil, Grant assumed that his "friend," although always a well-endowed redhead, was undoubtedly different every year.

Lily colored slightly and turned away from the look in his eyes. She began spooning coffee into a paper filter.

Lord, he must think I'm an unsophisticated country bumpkin, she thought. And she wasn't. Not usually, anyway. She didn't care a fig what Neil Baxter's sleeping arrangements were. Nor those of any of her other guests, for that matter. As long as they were discreet around the children, they had her blessing to do as they pleased with their sex lives.

"Neil and his friends always stay in cabin four," she said then, because she needed to say something to fill the small silence left by her verbal awkwardness. "That's the same one I've put you in. I'll have to make it up first, though. I wasn't expecting you until sometime tomorrow, so it isn't ready for guests." She risked a glance at him over her shoulder as she filled the glass coffeepot with water.

He was leaning back in the kitchen chair with his eyes half closed. His right leg was under the table, his left leg—the one that ended in a cast—stretched out to the side, toward the warmth that still emanated from the oven. The towel was hanging around his neck like a muffler, his hands lightly gripping the ends where they lay on his chest. The position stretched the flannel material of his plaid shirt across his shoulders, emphasizing his strength and power; it pulled the fabric of his jeans tight against his crotch and thighs, indicating his maleness; and it exposed the bare toes sticking out of the end of his cast, suggesting his vulnerability.

Lily turned back to the kitchen counter and poured the water into the coffee maker, telling herself that the only thing she'd noticed was the vulnerability. Evidence of anyone's pain, be it man or animal, always tugged her heartstrings. It was compassion she was feeling, nothing else. Just the simple compassion of one human being for another who was wet and tired and had been hurt. Being able to catalog the emotion made her feel much better.

"It'll be ready in a minute or two," she said, giving him a comforting smile as she flicked on the coffee maker. "In the meantime—" she opened another cupboard and took out a small stoneware plate "—how about a slice of fruit bread?"

Grant sat up straighter in the chair, looking toward the rows of bread cooling on the counter. "I thought you'd never ask."

Lily smiled at his eager expression. "I've got banana. Apple-cinnamon." She pointed at each kind as she named it. "Pumpkin. Carrot and raisin." There were nearly three dozen miniature loaves of each of the four kinds of bread.

"You must be real fond of the stuff."

"Oh, no, this isn't all for me." Her laugh was light and natural, the awkwardness of the past few minutes all but forgotten. She was on familiar ground now. Feeding people was her forte. "I bake for a restaurant here in Bend." She pulled a bread knife out of the wooden block on the counter. "What kind?"

"Ah..." His eyes ran greedily over the rows of bread. "Banana."

"Big slice or little slice?"

Grant gave her a little-boy smile. "Big."

"Big it is." Lily cut into the warm bread, releasing the sweet scent of bananas and vanilla into the warmth of the kitchen. The brewing coffee added its own rich fragrance to the room.

Grant sniffed appreciatively, smiling his thanks as she slid a plate and a mug of steaming coffee onto the table in front of him. He was even hungrier than he'd realized.

"Cream and sugar?"

"Neither, thanks." He took a big bite of the banana bread. "This is wonderful. *Wonderful.*" A quick swallow of coffee followed it down. "Really hits the spot."

Lily smiled her satisfaction; seeing someone enjoy her cooking always gave her a warm glow. "Help yourself to another piece if you want," she said, setting the loaf within easy reach on the table. "I'll just go get your cabin ready." She turned away, heading for the room off the kitchen that she had entered before. It housed her washer and dryer, her freezer, her shelves of home-canned produce and the bed linens and towels for the cabins.

"Hey." Grant's voice halted her in midstep. "You can't go out like that."

She looked back over her shoulder. "I'll put my rain-coat on first," she assured him. "It's on a hook right next to the back door. Galoshes, too."

Grant shook his head; that wasn't what he'd meant. "You've got blood on the hem of your robe."

Lily froze. "I've got *what*?"

"Blood—" he gestured with one hand "—on the hem of your robe."

"*My* blood?"

"Most likely."

Her face drained of all color, the forgotten pain of her grazed toes rushing back in full force. "Oh, Lord."

Grant's chair scraped against the floor as he came to his feet. "Hey, it's only a little bit of blood." His hand closed over her elbow. "Nothing to get excited about."

"No. No, of course not." Her voice was low, hesitant. "Just a little—" she gulped audibly "—blood."

Trust a woman to get bent out of shape over a little blood, Grant thought, but there was more amusement than ridicule in his expression. He grinned. "A tad squeamish, are we?"

"I . . ." She started to deny it, then stopped. It was obvious that she was. "Yes."

"Well, no problem. You took care of me." His big hands closed around her waist. "I'll take care of you."

In one powerful motion he lifted her, setting her on the one bit of counter space that wasn't covered by loaves of bread. Before she had time to object, he had yanked a paper towel off the roll next to the sink, wet it and was holding his hand out for her foot. Lily just looked at him, her fingers curled in a death grip around the tiled edge of the kitchen counter.

"Give me your foot." He wiggled his fingers demandingly.

Lily shook her head.

Ignoring her refusal, Grant reached out and took her bare foot in his hand. It was freezing. "What are you doing running around without your slippers on, anyway? It's the middle of winter."

"November," Lily muttered, feeling as if she might faint. Whether it was the sight of the blood on her toes or the feel of his big warm hand curled around her foot, she wasn't sure.

"What?"

"November isn't the middle of winter. It's— Ah!" She tried to jerk her foot out of his hand.

"Coward." He glanced up from his task and grinned at her. "I haven't even touched it yet." He took a firmer grip on her foot. "Now, hold still. This won't hurt a bit." He began gently dabbing the grazed places on the tops of her toes.

He was right; it didn't hurt. Not much, anyway. Lily gritted her teeth.

"Hardly any blood at all," he said soothingly, tossing the paper towel into the sink when he had finished with it. "I don't think it'll even need a Band-Aid." He ripped another towel from the roll and patted her toes dry. "There, now. See." He lifted his head to smile at her. "All better."

Their eyes met—and held. And this time it was Grant who was struck dumb.

Her eyes were blue. Not the clear, piercing blue of a summer sky or the intense, sultry blue of the Mediterranean at twilight, but something much softer and warmer. They made him think of a field of brilliant California lupin glimpsed through the mist of a summer rain; of watercolors by Monet; of fuzzy baby-blue blankets and fragile, speckled-blue robins' eggs and powder-blue velvet ribbons in a little girl's hair.

Soft.

Everything about her was soft; her eyes, wide and vulnerable as they returned his gaze; the pale gold of her lashes that were the same color as her hair; the creamy complexion that would have done credit to a fresh-faced model for a soap ad. And her lips...oh, yes, her lips were soft, too. Soft and pink and moist, slightly parted and just begging to be kissed. Unconsciously his hand tightened around her instep. "Lily?"

Lily didn't say a word. She just sat there on the edge of the kitchen counter, motionless, like a rabbit trapped in the headlights of a car. She couldn't form a coherent thought, let alone an answer to his unspoken question.

"Shall I kiss it and make it better?"

She still didn't say a word. She couldn't. But her eyes spoke volumes—and she would have been aghast if she could have seen what they said. *Oh, yes, please. Kiss it and make it better.*

Grant lifted her foot, lowering his head at the same time. Lily clutched the kitchen counter tighter and held her breath.

"Mommy, what are you doing?" The voice was high-pitched and sleepy. "Why are all the lights . on? Mommy?"

2

HE SHOULD'VE KNOWN she was married! His finely
honed so-called writer's instinct should have told him
so. But no, he'd let the lack of a wedding ring, not to
mention his preoccupation with a few rather detailed
fantasies about what she looked like under that blue
robe, blind him to all the other signs of the professional wife and mother.

There had been plenty of clues. If he'd been paying
attention to anything besides his libido he would have
seen them. She had the maternal persona down pat—
the comforting smile, the soothing words, that big old-
fashioned kitchen with gingham curtains at the window and the loaves of bread cooling on the counters.
Not to mention the way she'd made him feel all of ten
years old when she'd removed his jacket!

She hadn't been making a pass when she'd stood so
close and draped that towel over his head, she'd just
been trying to dry his hair. He was the one who had
tried to make something more out of it. And she'd let
him know, right away, that she wasn't interested.

Thinking back on it, Grant decided he'd never seen
a woman look so shocked by a teasing innuendo. Those
big blue eyes of hers had gotten as round as saucers.
And that blush! She'd looked like a naive teenager

who'd just been propositioned by the leader of the high school motorcycle gang. He grinned, wondering what she would have done if he'd given in to his baser instincts and buried his face between those tempting breasts of hers. Probably knocked his head off.

No, she hadn't tried to flirt with him at all. Except...well, except for that look she'd given him when he'd had her bare foot in his hand. That was a come-hither glance if he'd ever seen one. Wasn't it?

Grant folded his hands under his head and stared up into the dark above his bed. Hell, it must have been his imagination, he decided. God knows, he was tired enough to be imagining things. In any case, his imaginings had all been shot to hell when the first of Lily Talbot's three children had come into the kitchen.

Three kids, he thought, still finding it hard to believe. *She must have had the first one when she was fifteen!*

"Mommy, what are you doing?" the child had said, standing in the kitchen door in footed pink pajamas. She had a tattered stuffed dog in one hand. A striped blanket trailed from the other. "Why are all the lights on? Mommy?"

A boy of nine or ten followed hard on his sister's heels. "Lizzie woke me up," he announced through a huge yawn. His pajamas sported a picture of a Viking-like character on the chest with the words HE-MAN in bold yellow letters beneath it. He scratched his head sleepily and smiled sweetly at his mother. Grant might have been invisible, for all the attention the child paid him. "Can we have some hot chocolate?"

"I tried to tell 'em to go back to bed," said a third voice. "Lizzie came into our room and—" The young teenager came to an abrupt halt behind his brother and sister. "Mom?" He eyed the man holding his mother's foot in his hand with ill-concealed distrust. "Is everything okay?"

Lily jerked her foot out of Grant's hand and jumped off the kitchen counter before he could reach to lift her down. "Everything's fine." She scooted around Grant, a guilty flush coloring her cheeks. "Just fine."

"Who's he?" the elder boy asked, still eyeing Grant from beneath lowered brows. His eyes were the same color as his mother's but without the softness.

"This is our guest, Grant Saxon. You remember, Jeff, I told you we were expecting him. He arrived a little early, that's all." She stooped, bundling her daughter into her arms, and turned back to Grant. "These are my children," she said a little breathlessly. "This is Jeff." She indicated the elder boy with a nod of her head. "And Sean. And this—" she jiggled the little girl in her arms "—is Lizzie. Say hello to Mr. Saxon."

"'Lo," said Lizzie.

"Hi," said Sean.

"Why were you up on the counter?" said Jeff.

"I stubbed my toe," Lily explained. "Mr. Saxon was, um—" her blush intensified "—just wiping off the blood."

"How'd you stub your toe?" Jeff wanted to know.

"Oh, you know me," she said dismissively, bustling over to the kitchen table. "Running around barefoot."

She set her daughter in a chair. "Do all of you want chocolate before you go back to bed?"

"Yeah!" Both the younger children spoke at once.

"How come—" Jeff began, but Lily cut him off.

"Get out the saucepan for me, please, Jeff," she said, turning to open the refrigerator. She handed a plastic jug of milk to the boy. "You start the chocolate," she instructed him. "I'm just going to dash out and get Mr. Saxon's cabin made up."

"I can make up the cabin," Jeff began.

"There's no need for either of you to go out in this weather," Grant said. "Just give me the sheets or whatever. I can make it up myself."

"You're sure?" Lily looked doubtfully at the cast on his leg, her slender fingers brushing back the disordered curls that tumbled over her forehead. Her tongue snaked out to wet her lips. "That cast . . ."

"A broken leg doesn't make me a cripple," Grant said, thinking that if he didn't get out of the kitchen—soon!—he was going to grab Lily Talbot and do something that would *really* give her elder son something to scowl about.

"You're sure?" Lily said again, but she was already crossing the kitchen to open the utility room door. She got his jacket from the dryer, loaded his arms with crisp white sheets and fluffy yellow towels and sent him into the night with a haste that belied her own need to have him gone.

And now he found himself lying here in the bed he'd made himself, watching the flashes of lightning illuminate the beamed ceiling above his bed, and wondering what would have happened if Lily Talbot's three children hadn't come into the kitchen when they had. Would he be making love to her right now?

"Fat chance, Saxon," he muttered out loud.

More likely he'd be nursing a fat lip, he thought, a slight grin curving his lips. Because there was one thing he knew for damn sure: women like Miss—*Mrs.*—Lily Talbot didn't indulge in sexual games with men who weren't their husbands. No, sir, not women like her, born to be the wives and mothers of this world.

Of course, women like her usually wore wedding rings as wide as Band-Aids to let a man know they were strictly off-limits. So where the hell was Lily Talbot's official badge of wifedom? And where, come to think of it, was her husband?

There'd been the three kids but no husband. Odd. No, not odd, he argued with himself. There were any number of logical reasons why the man hadn't put in an appearance. Maybe he was on a business trip; maybe he worked the night shift somewhere so they could afford to feed those three kids; maybe he was sick in bed and so doped up with cold medicine that a missile launch wouldn't have wakened him. Maybe...

"Ah, what the hell do you care, Saxon?" Grant muttered. He rolled over, punching his pillow into a more comfortable position. "She's not your type, anyway."

He couldn't help but think, though, as he settled into sleep, that if a luscious little morsel like Lily Talbot was *his* wife, he sure as hell wouldn't be letting her open the door to strange men in the middle of the night.

HE WAS PULLED FROM SLEEP by the sound of someone knocking on the door of his cabin. Being one of those rare breed of outdoors enthusiasts who don't believe in rising with the sun, he tried to ignore it.

"Mr. Saxon? It's me, Lily Talbot. Are you awake?"

He grunted and rolled over, pulling the pillow over his head. No, he wasn't awake! It was too early to get up. Way too early. Besides, he was having the most wonderful dream.

She knocked again, her knuckles rattling the screen door against its frame. "Mr. Saxon?"

Grant pulled his head out from under the pillow. *Had* been having the most wonderful dream, he amended, scowling at the door. And she hadn't been calling him "Mr. Saxon," either. It had been "Oh, Grant darling." And she'd been moaning into his ear, not chirping like some damned bluebird through a closed door.

He lifted his wrist to eye level, trying to determine the time, but it was bare. "Must have left my watch in the bathroom," he mumbled disgustedly, snuggling his face back into the pillows. Whatever time it was, was too damned early, anyway. It was still gray outside; dawn had obviously not yet broken.

"Mr. Saxon? I'm sorry to bother you so early but I'm going into town."

Fine, he thought, *go into town. Just let me sleep.*

"Mr. Saxon?"

Geez, she's a persistent little— She reminded him of his mother trying to get him up in time for school when he was a kid. With a sigh, Grant pushed himself upright and swung his feet over the side of the bed. His cast clunked on the floor. "Yeah, I'm coming," he grumbled, running a hand through his tumbled hair as he looked around for something to put on. His jeans, if he remembered correctly, were lying on the bathroom floor, right where he had dropped them when he undressed last night. His backpack and suitcase were still out in the car.

Lily knocked again, louder this time.

"I'm coming!" he hollered. "Keep your shirt on." He got up from the bed, wrapping the bedspread around him as he rose. Tucking it around his waist, he dragged it across the room behind him as he fumbled toward the door. "You'd better have a pretty good reason for waking me up so early," he groused, peering at her through sleepy eyes.

She was bundled up against the cold, a navy parka zipped up to her chin, a matching ski cap pulled down to her eyebrows. "It's almost nine o'clock." Her tone was defensive. "I thought—hoped—you'd be up by now."

Grant grunted, squinting into the sky to verify her statement. It was filled with clouds, a fine drizzling mist all that was left of last night's storm. That explained the grayness of the morning but not the reason she had found it necessary to wake him up. "So why are you pounding on my door at 'almost nine o'clock'?" he grumbled. "I don't remember leaving a wake-up call."

"Well, no, you didn't. But I... That is..." Lily licked her lips nervously. It was obvious that he was wearing nothing but the bedspread wrapped around his lean waist. It hung on his hips—barely—leaving everything above it exposed. "I'm on my way into town," she hurried to explain. "Going to the grocery store. After I drop off my bread, that is."

"Uh-huh." Grant yawned, one hand absently scratching the furry mat of hair on his chest. "So what does that have to do with me?"

"Well, I, uh . . . I peeked into your Jeep and you don't seem to have brought any, um, supplies," she said, trying hard not to stare. She hadn't been this close to a bare male chest in, oh, longer than she could remember. And never one as broad and muscular as the one in front of her now.

His hand drifted lower, scratching the narrow line of hair just above his navel. It was the same chestnut brown as the hair on his head.

Lily swallowed, her eyes following the motion. His abdomen was washboard flat and as brown as tanned leather. There was a narrow strip of white showing where the bedspread dipped below his tan line. She forced her eyes back up. "I thought you might like me to pick up a few things for you. You know—" she shifted uncomfortably, trying not to notice the way his coppery male nipples contracted against the morning cold "—milk, bread. That sort of thing."

He yawned in response and hitched up his bedspread toga.

"Is that okay?"

"Oh, yeah." He yawned again. "Sure. That would be fine." He stepped back, pushing the screen door open to let her in. "Come on in and I'll give you some money."

He looked around distractedly. "If I can find my wallet."

Lily backed away from the door. Away from temptation. "No. No, that's okay. I'll just get a few things—just a few staples—and you can pay me later. I'll trust you for it." She started to turn away, then paused. "Is there anything you want especially?"

He stared at her upturned face, trying to think. Her lashes were jeweled with tiny raindrops, and the muffler wrapped around her neck matched the incredible color of her eyes. Her cheeks were flushed and rosy from the cold. He'd have to remember that for his next dream. Soft rosy cheeks and raindrops on her eyelashes.

"Mr. Saxon? Is there anything special you want?"

"What?" Grant gave himself a mental shake. "Oh, yeah. Sure." He thought a minute. "Coffee." He needed several cups before he could function in the morning. Intravenously, before he even got out of bed, would have been his preferred method. "Coffee would be wonderful. Any brand."

Lily nodded, then turned and ran across the graveled yard to the white Blazer that was parked at the back door of the lodge.

Grant stood at the open door and watched her hoist herself into the front seat. She gave a little hop just before she stepped up into the four-wheel-drive vehicle, an added boost that propelled her that extra needed inch upward. The motion did wonderful things to her derriere, causing it to wiggle enticingly under the tight fabric of her jeans.

She had great legs, long and slender in those tight jeans. But what the hell were those fuzzy things she was wearing? They encased her legs from boot top to mid-thigh, emphasizing their length and slenderness, showcasing that cute little fanny. He felt his body stir, hardening against his will.

Wife, he reminded himself sternly. *Mother*.

He stepped back, slamming the cabin door to shut out the sight of her. "You'd better get dressed before you freeze to death, Saxon," he said out loud, trying to ignore the fact that his body was anything but cold.

BY THE TIME Lily got back from town, Grant had showered and dressed and would have willingly sold his next byline for a single cup of coffee. He was out the door of his cabin and halfway across the graveled yard before she had brought the Blazer to a complete stop behind the lodge.

"Hi," she said brightly, jumping down from the driver's seat as he opened the door for her. It was easy to be bright and cheerful—now. He was fully clothed. Besides, she had given herself a stern talking-to on the drive home from town. There would be no more drooling over half-naked guests. "Are you awake now?"

"Awake and starving." He was gazing longingly at the bags of groceries in the back of the Blazer. A can of coffee was sticking out of the top of one of them.

Lily smiled, recognizing the look on his face. Her son Sean wore that exact same expression when he was waiting for her chocolate chip cookies to cool. "Well, come on into the kitchen," she invited, leaning into the back seat for a bag of groceries, "and I'll whip you up some bacon and eggs."

Grant took the bag from her. "That wasn't a hint."

"I didn't think it was." She reached for another bag. "Do you like pancakes?"

"Pancakes?" He took the second bag of groceries from her. "You're offering me pancakes?"

"Made-from-scratch buttermilk pancakes, dripping with melted butter and warm maple syrup. A side order of crisp bacon. Two eggs any way you like them. Ice-cold orange juice and—" she hauled another bag out of the back seat "—coffee."

Grant licked his lips. "Who do I have to kill?"

Lily laughed. "No one. Just bring the rest of those groceries in for me and—" She glanced at the worn cast on his leg. "Can you handle the groceries with that?"

"Sure. No problem."

"It won't be too much for you?"

"I don't carry groceries with my feet."

Lily smiled. "Well, okay then, bring the groceries in and we'll call an even trade for breakfast." She paused at the back door, the bag she carried balanced on an out-thrust hip. "The one with the can of Maxwell House sticking out of the top is yours," she said. "I had the cashier ring it up separately, so the receipt's in the bag. If there's anything you don't want, we'll deduct it from what you owe me." She turned and reached for the doorknob, speaking to him over her shoulder. "I wasn't sure what you'd consider staples so I just— Oh!" The door opened inward without her pushing it. "Tim." A smile lit up her face. "I thought you'd be gone by now."

This must be the husband, thought Grant, looking him over with a critical eye. He was a good-looking cuss—there was no getting around that. But his dark curly hair was too long for respectability and the red bandana tied around his forehead, Indian fashion, was a bit too hip for the father of three kids. Come to think of it, he didn't look old enough to be the father of three kids. Or responsible enough, either. Definitely not the kind of man he expected a woman like Lily Talbot to have married. He had been imagining a nine-to-fiver in a three-piece suit, or a hardworking blue-collar man, not an overaged hippie.

"Fixing that flue took longer than I thought," the man was saying to Lily. "Then I figured I might as well check the other two while I was at it. It'll save time in the long run."

"I'm sure it will." She caught the speculative glance that passed between the two men and hurried to make introductions. "Tim, this is Grant Saxon. He's staying in cabin four. Mr. Saxon—"

"Grant," he corrected.

"Grant, then," Lily said. "Grant, this is Tim Wade." She put a fond hand on the younger man's arm. "Our handyman here at Talbot's. If you have any problems with anything while you're here—leaky ceilings or you need more firewood or something—Tim's the man to call. He lives over in cabin six."

Handyman? Grant thought, nodding a greeting over the grocery sacks in his arms. *Not husband?* Then,

*where in hell was her husband if she needed a handy-
man on the place?*

"Pleased to meet you," Tim said politely before
turning his attention back to Lily. "Listen, babycakes,
I gotta run. Mrs. Dodd's expecting me to put together
the display shelves in her new shop." He dropped a
quick peck on her upturned cheek. "If you need me for
anything, you can reach me there. I left the number on
the bulletin board."

"Have you had breakfast?" she called as he headed
across the yard to the black four-wheel-drive pickup
parked in front of cabin six. Orange flames flickered
down each side and across the top of the cab.

"Yes, mother." He tossed them a careless wave as he
drove out of the yard. There was a roar as he acceler-
ated, the squeal of tires as he hit the wet pavement, then
silence.

Grant looked at her over the top of the grocery sacks.
"Babycakes?"

"I know." She grimaced comically, her eyes meeting
his in a look of adult understanding. "Awful, isn't it?
But he's dependable and he works cheap." She smiled
and shrugged, shifting the bag of groceries to her other
hip. "Well, come on in."

She bustled through the utility room and into the
kitchen ahead of him. "Just let me get some of these
things put away first, then I'll put the coffee on. Okay?"

"No hurry," he lied. "Where do you want these?"

Lily glanced into the bag he held. "Just set it on the
counter over there. It's just baking supplies. Nothing
that has to be put away immediately."

Grant did as she'd directed and went out for another load, and then another. By the time he had finished bringing in all her groceries, the welcome scent of coffee and frying bacon permeated the kitchen and she was whipping buttermilk and flour into a ceramic bowl. A place had been set for him at one end of the long trestle table, complete with place mat, cutlery and a yellow flowered cloth napkin.

"You didn't have to go to all this trouble."

"No trouble." Lily smiled at him over her shoulder. "Have a seat," she invited, turning back to the griddle as she tested it for temperature. Droplets of water skittered over the surface. She poured six silver-dollar-size rounds of batter onto it, then turned to him with the coffeepot in hand. "Here you go." She filled his cup with the fragrant brew. "Coffee."

Grant picked it up as if it were a life-giving elixir. He sniffed it first, as was his habit, then took a sip. It was strong, hot and satisfying.

"Think you'll live now?" Lily teased, turning back to the stove to tend to the pancakes.

"I'll survive. I don't start to actually live until after the second cup."

"There's plenty." She cracked an egg against the side of the stove. "How do you like your eggs?"

"Over easy, please," he said, watching her as she broke two eggs onto the griddle. That done, she turned the pancakes to cook on the other side, then transferred the bacon to a paper towel to drain. All her movements were neat, economical and precise; the lady knew her way around a kitchen.

She had taken off her knit cap, replacing it with a wide barrette that held her hair in a low ponytail on the back of her neck. She had exchanged her navy parka for an apron. It was a plain white chef's apron with long ties that went twice around her slender waist before tying in a little bow at the back. The ends trailed over the seat of her jeans. She was still wearing those fuzzy things on her legs. They were easily one of the sexiest items of clothing he had ever seen on a woman.

"What the hell do you call those things?"

Lily turned the eggs. "What things?" she asked, bending over to take a plate out of the warming oven.

Grant's eyes remained riveted on the seat of her jeans. "Those sweater things on your legs."

She stacked the pancakes onto the plate. "Leg warmers." One egg went on either side of the pancakes. "Why?"

Leg warmers, huh? He could think of another part of his anatomy they were warming. He reached for his coffee cup, cradling it in both hands. It was either that or her bottom. "Just wondering." He took a sip of his coffee. "I thought only ballet dancers and aerobics fanatics wore 'em."

"I like them because they're so cozy in this weather." Crisp slices of bacon joined the eggs and pancakes. She set the filled platter in front of him with a flourish. "There!" She placed small pitchers of warmed maple syrup and melted butter within easy reach. "Dig in."

It was the kind of meal his mother had always set in front of him—a plate heaping with whatever was being served. She hovered like his mother, too, watching anxiously as he took the first bite, then smiling with satisfaction when he signaled his pleasure by taking another.

Mother, he reminded himself, picking up a piece of crisp bacon in his fingers. *Lily Talbot is the mother of three kids.*

The trouble was, she didn't look like the mother of anyone. Even in her plain white apron and with a spatula in her hand, she looked like every man's dream of the perfect bedmate.

Stray wisps and tendrils of hair had escaped her ponytail to fall against her temples and down the sides of her neck, as if they had been tousled in love play. Her cheeks were flushed from the heat of the stove, but it was easy to imagine that the heat of passion had made them that way. Her lips were rosy and smiling. Her eyes were soft and blue and anxious to please.

She was wearing something that looked like the top part of a set of thermal underwear as a blouse. It was pink with tiny multicolored flowers embroidered around the neckline; it was modest, covering her from collarbone to wrist; and it clung to every curving line of her torso.

Why the hell couldn't she look like what she was?

"Aren't you eating anything?" he said almost irritably.

Lily shook her head and turned away to get the coffeepot. His cup was only half full. "I ate breakfast with the kids before they went to school."

"Hubby, too?"

It took her a minute to get his meaning. "Oh, no." She stood with one hand on the back of his chair, the other holding the coffeepot suspended over his cup. "No husband. I'm divorced."

Divorced. A slow smile spread over Grant's face. A smile he wasn't even aware of. Then, inordinately pleased by the information and completely forgetting her three kids, he reached up and put his hand on the back of her neck. Without another thought he pulled her down to meet his kiss.

3

SURPRISE HELD Lily stock-still for a second, unable to either respond to or repulse the man who was kissing her. She could feel his lips moving on hers, could feel his hand on the back of her neck, but somehow she couldn't quite connect those sensations with herself. It had been a long time since she had been kissed. A very long time. Which wasn't surprising, she thought, considering her three-year-old divorce—and the fact that she wasn't a particularly kissable woman, anyway.

Well, okay, kissable, she amended. *You didn't get three children without being at least kissable.*

But she certainly wasn't the kind of woman who inspired men to rash acts of passion in the middle of the kitchen on a rainy Friday morning. She was a mother; a member of the PTA; a person who canned her own vegetables and baked her own bread and knitted sweaters at night while she sat at the kitchen table and supervised the children's homework. Just a plain, ordinary, run-of-the-mill *hausfrau,* she thought, not some femme fatale who caused strange men to kiss her for no reason.

Grant's mouth opened under hers then, his hand tightening on the back of her neck to pull her closer. Lily abruptly ceased trying to think at all. She simply responded. Her hand fluttered up from the back of the kitchen chair to lightly, hesitantly touch the unruly curls at the nape of his neck. Her lips parted. She sighed.

It was a small breathy sigh, hardly more than a whisper of sound, but Grant felt it all the way down to his toes. His body hardened instantly, and he had an intense urge to pull her down into his lap and make her sigh again. Make her gasp. Make her moan. Make her—

Dammit, Saxon, what the hell do you think you're doing?

He let go of her neck. "Great breakfast," he said, his mouth only inches from hers. "Thanks."

Lily straightened slowly, her hand lifting from his hair to press against the bodice of her apron. Her soft blue eyes were wide and slightly unfocused. Her mouth was as lush as a ripe plum.

Grant looked down at his plate, away from the temptation she unwittingly offered him. "It's not often I get eggs cooked exactly the way I like them. And these pancakes—" He forked a bite into his mouth, holding his free hand up with the thumb and forefinger circled. "Perfect."

Lily wasn't quite sure what to say to that. What could you say to a man who kissed you practically senseless one second and then calmly complimented your cooking the next? "I'm, ah . . . I'm glad everything's cooked to your satisfaction." She lifted the coffeepot slightly, hoping he wouldn't notice the way her hand was trembling. "More coffee?"

Hell, yes, he wanted more coffee. He wanted gallons of coffee. "No, thanks." He picked up his half-empty cup. "This is fine."

Lily turned back to the stove. "Would you like more pancakes?" she said, taking refuge in the familiar. "Another egg?"

His empty cup clinked against the saucer as he put it down. "No, thanks. I'm stuffed to the gills." His knife and fork clattered as he laid them across his plate. "That was a great breakfast."

Lily continued to face the stove, scraping hot grease off the griddle with the edge of the spatula. "I'm glad you liked it."

"I did, indeed. Best breakfast I've had in a long time. Eggs were perfect. Bacon was nice and crisp." *Oh, shut up, Saxon,* he told himself irritably. *You sound like a slimy snake-oil salesman trying to butter her up.* His chair scraped against the floor as he pushed it back. "Well, I guess I'd better get going. Got to get started on that article." He stood up. "How much do I owe you?"

Lily risked a quick glance over her shoulder. "Owe me?" Did he want to pay for his breakfast?

He nodded toward the grocery sacks still sitting on the tiled counter. "For the groceries."

"Oh, the groceries." She set down the spatula, wiping her hands on a dish towel tucked into the waistband of her apron as she crossed the room. Her arm brushed his as she reached for the grocery sack. They both pretended it hadn't. "The receipt's in the bag somewhere," she murmured, shifting a few items around in an effort to locate it. It wasn't under the can of coffee or stuck to the side of the package of sliced cheese.

He moved forward, looking over her shoulder as she searched for it. "Is that it?" His big hand appeared over her shoulder, pointing.

"No, that's a coupon that—" He was close. Too close. She could practically feel him breathing down the back of her neck. "Look, why don't you take the groceries back to your cabin. You'll find the receipt when you put them away." She lifted the bag from the counter and turned, thrusting it into his arms. "You can pay me later, okay?"

His hands curled around the sack, the backs of his fingers brushing against her stomach as he lifted it out of her arms. "Okay."

Their eyes met. Soft, vulnerable blue; bold, sparkling brown. Something indefinable sizzled between them in that moment. Something warm and sweet and filled with unrecognized longing. They both looked away.

"Well, thanks for cooking my breakfast."

"You're welcome."

"It really was delicious. You're a great cook."

"Thank you. I like cooking."

"It shows."

"Thank you," she said again. She didn't know what else to say.

"Well . . ." He felt like a teenager on his first date, wondering how to go about getting a kiss before he said goodbye. "I guess I'd better be going. Get this stuff put away before it spoils."

"Yes," she agreed. "I guess you'd better."

He backed away a few steps, then turned and walked to the door, his cast clunking against the worn wooden boards of the kitchen floor with every other footfall. The outside screen door banged shut behind him.

Lily sank onto the chair he had vacated, fizzling like a balloon with a slow leak. She propped her elbow on the table and pressed her forehead into her palm. "Oh, Lord."

Why had he kissed her? And why, oh why, had she reacted like some desperate sex-starved divorcée?

She hadn't thought it was possible, but she'd obviously been too long without a man in her life. Way too long, judging from her reaction to a simple thank-you kiss. If that's what it had been? Oh, yes, she decided, that's what it had been, all right. Look how fast he'd backed off when she'd tried—however unintentionally!—to make it into more. He'd been almost as embarrassed as she was. Hemming and hawing like a nervous schoolboy until he could make his escape. He'd probably thought she was going to jump him.

Lord, she felt like such a fool. A stupid fool for turning a simple, uncomplicated thank-you kiss into—

She lifted her head, a sudden thought occurring to her.

Had it really been so simple? So uncomplicated? She reached out, absently running the tip of her finger over the rim of his empty coffee cup as she pondered the question. Certainly nobody she knew put quite that much . . . that much *heat* into a simple thank-you kiss.

Of course, she reminded herself, he *was* from California. And a friend of Neil Baxter's. Those two facts alone were probably enough to explain his overly intimate thank-you. Given the chance, he probably kissed every woman he met exactly the same way. And it probably meant nothing.

Of course it meant nothing, she told herself. To him, and certainly to her. The whole silly incident wasn't worth another thought.

She stood up with a brisk air of purpose and carried his empty plate and coffee cup to the sink. Her eyes, as always, were drawn to the wide, gingham-hung window above it.

It was raining again—the sky low and gray, the fine mist of the morning turned to a depressing drizzle. Dripping, rain-soaked pine trees ringed the yard, standing sentinel behind and between the semicircle of cabins that fanned out behind the lodge. There was a lazy spiral of smoke drifting upward from the chimney pipe of cabin six, evidence of the slow-burning fire that Tim had left in his Franklin stove. Light shone from the windows of cabin four, reflecting off the shallow puddles that dotted the gravel drive between it and the lodge. She watched the raindrops spatter on the puddles as she rinsed the dishes, wondering if Grant had taken the time to dry off his cast when he got back to his cabin. It would be ruined if he hadn't.

THE FIRST THING Grant did when he got back to his cabin was head for the pullman kitchen to make a much-needed pot of coffee. He spent a few frustrating minutes banging cupboard doors, looking for the pot. And then it took him a minute more to recognize it for what it was when he did find it. In the modern world of Mr. Coffee, it wasn't often you ran across an aluminum percolator with a metal strainer and a glass knob on top so you could watch the coffee perk.

He wasn't interested in watching it perk, however—he was only interested in drinking it. Soon. Maybe coffee would clear his head and stop the parade of graphic, highly erotic pictures that had begun forming in his mind the second she had opened her mouth to his kiss.

What the hell were you thinking of, Saxon? Kissing her like that?

He stopped fumbling with the coffeepot and thought about it for a minute. What had he been thinking about? Certainly not the fact that she had three kids. And not the fact that she wasn't his type, either. She was too maternal, too... The memory of how she had looked, standing there in her kitchen, with her jeans hugging her cute little backside and soft tendrils of blond hair falling out of her ponytail, brought a rush of heat to his loins.

"Get off it, Saxon," he said aloud, disgusted with his feeble attempt at self-deception. "A woman who looks like that has always been your type."

So okay, he thought, shrugging as he spooned coffee into the metal filter. Maybe she was his type—physically. He was as susceptible as the next guy to a beautiful blue-eyed blonde. So what? Did that mean he had to give in to his baser instincts the first chance he got? Didn't he have any control?

"Stupid question, Saxon," he muttered to himself. He fitted the lid onto the coffeepot, slamming it down with the flat of his hand, and shoving the plug into the wall socket.

His control was obviously zilch. Or it had been a little while ago. But, hell, it'd been—what?—four, maybe five weeks since he and Marcie had gone their separate ways. His lack of control was understandable.

But it damned sure wouldn't be repeated.

Coming on to a woman like Lily Talbot was just asking for trouble. Even an idiot could see that she wasn't the casual-playmate type; not the kind of woman you could share a few laughs with and then move on, with no recriminations and no regrets on either side. No, sir. A woman like Lily Talbot stood for permanence and responsibility. Commitment with a capital *C*. And, to paraphrase an old saying, he wasn't ready to be committed. Not now. Probably not ever. Certainly not to a little mother-hen homebody with three kids, not even if she *did* have the cutest little tush he'd ever seen and the sweetest, softest mouth he'd ever tasted.

The only trouble was, how was he going to keep himself from tasting it again, just as soon as he got the chance?

He thought about it for a second, drumming his fingers on the countertop as he waited for the coffee to perk. The answer, he decided, was not to give himself another chance. Just stay away from her, that's all. Just stay the hell away from her.

He stopped drumming his fingers and glared at the hapless pot. "Perk, dammit!"

GRANT DID HIS LEVEL BEST to follow his own advice. He spent the rest of the day in town, visiting the chamber of commerce, talking to a couple of local white-water rafting companies and taking a tour of a camping out-fitter who used llamas instead of packhorses for treks into the Oregon backwoods. He even had dinner in Bend, thinking to save himself from having to decline Lily's invitation to dinner at the lodge.

He needn't have bothered, he realized later. She was obviously doing her best to keep out of his way, too. There were no more early-morning wake-up calls, no more offers to run errands for him, no more invita-tions to breakfast after her kids had gone to school.

Not that they'd gone to school either of the past two days, Grant reminded himself. Kids usually didn't on weekends. He'd seen them a few times on Saturday from the window in front of the desk where he'd set up his battered old portable and the preliminary research material he'd gathered on his trip into town.

The elder boy—Jeff, she'd called him—was already a head taller than his mother. Grant judged him to be about thirteen, certainly no older than fourteen, with the scrawny, all-hands-and-feet build that boys that age were apt to have. He seemed to have a lot of chores around the place. Grant had watched him haul suit-cases and wood for the two old geezers who had checked into cabin one, chop kindling for his mother and reprimand his little sister when she came outside without her rain hat or galoshes. Not, of course, that she'd paid any more attention to him than any other little sister did to her big brother.

She'd stuck out her tongue, pushing rain-damp blond curls off her cheek with her palm, and dashed off to stamp around in the puddles. It took a stern word from her mother to call her indoors again.

"Elizabeth, come back in the house."

Elizabeth continued splashing gleefully through the puddles, kicking up showers of water with her pink plaid sneakers, seemingly oblivious to her mother's presence on the back porch.

"Elizabeth Allison Talbot," she warned, raising her voice slightly. "I'm not kidding."

The child looked up at her mother with an angelic little smile on her face—a rain-soaked water sprite in a shiny red mackintosh. "What, Mommy?"

"You know what," Lily said, not the least bit fooled by the innocent smile of her six-year-old daughter. She held open the door. "Back in the house before you turn into a human ice cube."

The child's shoulders slumped dejectedly, one sneakered foot tracing a slow circle in the shallow puddle. "I'm not cold," she said mutinously, her lower lip stuck out in a pout.

"I don't care if you're not cold. *I'm* cold. And your feet are soaking wet."

"She's being a brat." Lily's middle child, Sean, came out on the porch to offer his opinion.

The water sprite turned into a termagant. "I am not!"

"Are too!"

"Am not!"

"Are—"

"That's enough, both of you! Sean, go back inside, please. We don't need your input right now."

Sean went back inside without another word.

Lily pinned her daughter with a look. "And as for you, young lady, I'd suggest you get yourself in here. Now."

Elizabeth hesitated.

"Neither of us will like what happens if I have to come after you."

Realizing that she'd tested her mother enough for one day, Elizabeth relented and went inside.

Lily smiled at her elder son. "Why don't you just leave that for now, honey?"

"I was gonna chop some more kindling."

Lily shook her head. "We've got enough for tonight. Come on in now. You're almost as wet as Lizzie."

"But—"

"No buts. You can chop kindling tomorrow if we need it." She cast a prayerful glance skyward. "Maybe it'll stop raining by then."

He'd been right about her all along, Grant thought with a sense of satisfaction as he watched her herd her children in out of the rain. Lily Talbot was a mother hen. Not his type at all. Thank God. Now if he could only convince his libido of that. . . .

THE FOLLOWING MORNING brought a partial answer to Lily's prayer. It stopped raining around eleven o'clock, a pale winter sun breaking through the gray clouds, making the still-dripping pine trees sparkle as if they were covered with tiny iridescent jewels.

Tempted by the break in the weather, Grant ambled out onto the tiny front porch of his cabin, his third cup of coffee in hand, and settled down on the top step to enjoy the beauty of the day.

It was peaceful on the porch, and almost warm with the frail November sun shining on his outstretched legs and the bare toes exposed by his cast. The soft plop-plop of the rain dripping off the trees and the steeply pitched roofs of the buildings made an oddly musical sound, he thought, like a hundred tiny drums being beaten in slow cadence by a hundred tiny soldiers. Occasional bursts of birdsong filled the air, squirrels chattered, and somewhere far off in the distance he could hear the whirring sound of a chain saw in use. He breathed deeply, savoring the combined smells of the rain-washed woods, the cup of coffee in his hand, the faint scent of wood smoke that drifted on the air.

Neil had been right, he decided, leaning back on his elbows. He'd needed some time away from the rat race. Some time off to recharge his batteries and just relax for a change.

Always supposing, he thought then, grinning, that it was humanly possible to relax with a temptation like Lily Talbot within arm's reach.

He glanced toward the lodge as he thought of her, wondering suddenly at the silence that surrounded it. Yesterday morning there had been shouts and laughter and banging doors and rock music coming from an upstairs window from dawn to dusk. Now it was silent, not even a whisper of smoke curling from the chimney to tell him that someone was home. Just as he was thinking about getting up to investigate the situation, Lily's white Blazer pulled into the gravel driveway.

The family had obviously just come back from church; the boys looked uncomfortable in their navy slacks and "good" sweaters; Elizabeth looked like a little princess in patterned tights and shiny black Mary Janes, a red corduroy coat buttoned up to her chin; Lily looked anything but motherly in a soft gray sweater dress that showed her slender figure to advantage. She wore misty gray stockings, too, and high-heeled pumps, and her hair was done up in some sort of a bun, with soft wavy tendrils falling down around her neck and ears.

Ah, sweet Lily, Grant thought, his eyes following every graceful move she made as she waved the two boys into the house to change their clothes. *What a temptation you are.*

Unaware that she was being watched, Lily turned back to the Blazer to help her daughter out. The movement positioned her with her back to Grant, her hips out-thrust as she leaned into the car. The soft fabric of her dress pulled taut across her fanny, outlining its delectable shape as she handed the child out of the vehicle.

Cutest little tush in the world, Grant thought, feeling his body stir to life.

For a moment he considered getting up and going back inside his cabin where it was safe. But that would be rude, he decided. Unforgivably rude. He was, after all, renting the cabin from her. The only polite thing to do was to go over and say hello. No harm in a simple greeting. Besides, he still owed her the money for the groceries.

He set his coffee cup on the step and heaved himself to his feet. "Hi," he called, weaving his way around the puddles that still dotted the drive, trying to save the bedraggled cast on his left foot from any further water damage.

Lily's head whirled around at the sound of his voice. "Oh, Mr. Saxon." *Be cool, Lily,* she cautioned herself. *Calm and collected and cool.* She turned toward him, one hand still holding on to her daughter's, a brave smile on her lips. "Hello."

"Been to church?"

She nodded, her eyes not quite meeting his. "Yes."

"Nice sermon?"

"Yes, very nice, thank you." Seeking a distraction, any distraction, she looked down at her daughter. "Lizzie, say hello to Mr. Saxon."

"Hello." Elizabeth gave him a sweet smile. "I've been to church, too," she said importantly. "Our sunny-school teacher told us all about Noah's ark." She peered up at Grant from under spun-gold lashes. "Do you know about Noah's ark?"

Grant hesitated, not quite sure how to respond to the child. Would she be upset if he said he did?

"Lizzie, I'm sure Mr. Saxon doesn't want to hear about Sunday school right now."

Elizabeth's cherubic little face clouded.

"No. No, that's all right," he lied quickly. "I'd love to hear about Noah's ark."

Elizabeth smiled and wriggled out of her mother's hold. "It rained an' rained," she began in a hushed voice. "Just like now. An' Noah had to build a big ark. That's the biggest boat there ever was," she added, spreading her arms wide. "Forty cubes by forty cubes. An' all the animals got on it so they wouldn't drown. They had to line up in two rows, boys 'n' girls, just like Mrs. Willis makes us do after recess at kiddy-garden. An' they stayed on it for a long, long time. An' then it stopped raining an' they all got out and went back to the woods and ate olives. The end," she said, so he'd know. "Did you like it?"

Grant had a hard time hiding his grin. "Best story I've heard in a long time."

"Me an' Sean are gonna build an ark," she confided, all dimples and wide blue eyes as she looked up at him. "We're gonna get the nails an' stuff from Tim. Tim lives over there." She pointed at the last cabin in the row. "He's our friend an'—"

"Okay, Elizabeth," Lily interrupted. "That's enough. You've told Mr. Saxon all about Noah's ark." She put her hand on the child's shoulders and turned her toward the lodge. "It's time for you to go in and change your clothes."

"But Mommy..."

"You want to help Sean build that ark, don't you?"

Elizabeth nodded.

"Then inside and change."

Elizabeth bolted for the back door.

"I'm sorry about that." Lily motioned toward the re-treating figure of her daughter. "She thinks everyone is just dying to hear what she has to say."

"I enjoyed it," Grant said, surprised to realize that he meant it. "She's a real charmer."

Lily laughed. "She's a ham."

He shook his head. "A charmer," he insisted. "Just like her mother." *Where the hell did that come from?*

Lily's eyes widened. *Charming?* they said. *Me?*

"You," Grant said, as if she'd spoken the thought out loud.

Lily blushed, the soft color creeping up from under the high neck of her gray dress like dawn stealing over the morning sky. Before he could stop himself, Grant reached out and gently brushed the backs of his fingers against her flushed cheek. Lily sucked in her breath and held it, waiting for what he would do next.

The screen door squealed on its hinges. "Mom, Dad's on the phone," her elder son hollered from the back porch. With ill-disguised distrust, he eyed the man touching his mother. "He's calling about Thanksgiving."

Grant's hand dropped back to his side.

Lily sighed. "Tell him I'll be right there." She gave Grant an apologetic, embarrassed little shrug. "I'm being paged," she said, half turning toward the lodge.

"Wait."

Lily paused expectantly.

"I haven't paid you yet. For the groceries."

"Oh." She waved a graceful hand, wondering how he could think of money and groceries when her own brain had turned to warm mush. "There's no hurry. Really."

"No, I already wrote out the check. Been carrying it around—" Grant stuffed two fingers into the tight front pocket of his jeans "—waiting for a chance to give it to you. Here." He held it out to her.

"Mom, it's long-distance!" Jeff called from the porch, his voice two shades away from an impatient whine.

"Yes, I'm coming." Her fingers closed over the folded scrap of paper. It was warm. As his fingers had been against her cheek. "Thank you," she murmured softly.

"Thank *you*," he returned just as softly. He didn't release his hold on the check.

"Mom!"

She frowned in annoyance at the repeated summons but didn't turn around to answer it. "I have to go in."

"Yes," he agreed.

Still neither of them moved. Their fingertips were just touching, their eyes meeting over their outstretched hands.

"He's gonna hang up," Jeff warned, his tone gone past impatience to adolescent challenge.

"*All right*, Jeff. I'm coming." She pulled the crumpled check from Grant's fingers. "Thank you," she said again.

Grant stood where he was for a moment, watching her walk away from him. The high heels forced her to step carefully over the graveled surface of the yard, exaggerating the feminine sway of her hips under the gray dress as she mounted the steps to the porch. She said something to her tall young son that brought a quick frown and a reluctant nod, and then the door closed behind them. Grant turned back toward his cabin, his day gone suddenly as dreary as the cloud-covered sky had been before the sun came out. He wasn't inside more than ten minutes, however, before there was a knock at the door.

"Come on in," he called irritably, busy pouring himself another cup of coffee. "It's open."

A blond head emerged around the edge of the door, then a pair of bright blue eyes and a wiry, compact body clad in Levi's and a kelly-green parka. "Hi." A tentative gap-toothed smile accompanied the greeting. "I'm Sean."

Grant's irritability left him as suddenly as it had come; all three of Lily's kids looked remarkably like her. Deliberately not pausing to wonder why that cheered him, he leaned his hips back against the kitchen counter and took a sip of his coffee. "What can I do for you, Sean?" he asked, motioning the boy in with his free hand.

"Mom sent me over to give you this," he said from the doorway. He held up a narrow oblong box.

"What is it?"

"Garbage bags."

"Garbage bags? What for?"

"For your cast," Sean said, as if Grant should have known without having to ask. "To keep it dry. You put one over—" He stumbled forward suddenly, as if he had been hit from behind. "Lizzie!" he bellowed, rounding on his younger sister. "Go away. Mom said you're not supposed to bother Mr. Saxon."

"I'm not botherin' him," Elizabeth said indignantly, elbowing her way into the cabin. She had exchanged her red coat and Mary Janes for denim overalls and sneakers. A bright red sweatshirt was tied around her waist. "I brought him some rubber ban's." She held her chubby fist under her brother's nose and opened it. "See? Mommy gave 'em to me."

"Give them to me," Sean demanded, making a grab for her wrist. "*I'll* give them to Mr. Saxon."

Elizabeth's fist snapped closed. "No!" She put her hand behind her back. "I want to."

"*Lizzie.*" Sean's voice carried an ominous warning.

"It's all right, Sean." Grant put his coffee cup down and pushed away from the counter, deciding it was time to do something before World War III started. "Here, Lizzie, you can give the rubber bands to me," he said, holding out his hand.

The little girl shot a triumphant look at her brother and bounced across the room to Grant. "They're all big ones," she said, dumping them into his hand. "Mommy picked them out 'specially."

"Thank you." He looked from one child to the other. "What am I supposed to do with them?"

Elizabeth and Sean looked at each other, allies again in the face of such monumental ignorance. Elizabeth shook her curly blond head and tsked audibly. "Sit down here," she ordered, dragging one of the two chairs away from the small kitchen table. Her expression was one of pure female exasperation with the whole helpless male sex.

They begin young, Grant thought, stifling a grin as he obeyed her. She reminded him of Lily when she had been drying his hair. Mother hens, both of them. It was almost endearing.

"You have to lift your foot *up*," she instructed, tugging his knee.

"Oh, sorry."

"That's okay," she said magnanimously, her little hand behind the bend of his knee as if she were holding his foot off the floor while Sean struggled to slip the plastic garbage bag over his cast. "You put it over your cast, see? So it won't get wetter." She sighed impatiently. "Where's the rubber ban'?"

Grant opened his hand. She looked the rubber bands over carefully before picking one, then squatted down in front of him, shouldering her brother out of the way to do so. "Lift up your foot more," she ordered.

The rubber band was a bit unruly in her hands, catching on the plastic bag as she tried to hold it stretched open and slip it over his foot at the same time. For a moment Grant was silent, afraid he might hurt her feelings if he attempted to help her, afraid she would hurt herself if he didn't. Sean had no such qualms.

"Lizzie, you're doing it wrong."

She shot him a glance out of the corner of narrowed cornflower-blue eyes, but otherwise ignored him. The rubber band snapped against her fingers.

Grant dropped his handful of rubber bands on the table. "Here, better let me do it," he said, taking it from her. "I should know how to do it by myself, don't you think?" he added, before she could object. He settled the rubber band around the top edge of his cast. "How's that?"

Elizabeth looked it over with a critical eye, then reached out and patted it into place. "Very good," she said in obvious imitation of her mother.

Grant lost the struggle to hide his grin; she was so damned cute! "Thank you, Lizzie. And thank you, too, Sean. My cast was getting pretty soggy."

Elizabeth stood up then and leaned against Grant's knee. "Sean had a broken leg once."

"Really?" Unused to children, Grant wasn't quite sure how to react to their conversational gambits. It was sort of like dealing with the natives of an unfamiliar culture, he thought—like the time he'd tried to converse with an Amazon River boatman without the help of an interpreter. "How did it happen, Sean?" he asked with real interest.

"I was climbing that big pine tree by the edge of the driveway— You know, the one with the swing on it? Well, my foot slipped on the branches and I fell."

"He broke his leg in *two* places," Elizabeth added, unwilling to be left out. "He got knocked out an' was all bloody all over his leg an' Mommy thought he was dead. I did, too," she confided. "But then he woked up an' started crying an' screaming, so we knew he wasn't dead."

Sean shot her a furious glance.

"I did some crying and screaming myself when I broke my ankle," Grant said, correctly interpreting the look.

Sean stopped glaring at his sister. "You *did*?"

"Sure." Grant nodded. "It hurt like hel—heck."

Sean edged onto the other kitchen chair and leaned his elbows on the table. "How did you break it?" he wanted to know.

"I was climbing El Capitan and a couple of my pitons pulled loose. I fell about twenty feet before I slammed into the face of the cliff."

Sean's eyes were round with admiration. *"Wow."*

"What's a pee-ton?" Elizabeth asked.

"It's a..." He hesitated. How much explanation would a little girl like her understand? "It's a little metal spike that you hammer into the rock to hold the rope when you're climbing so you won't fall," he said at last.

"Climbing what?"

Sean rolled his eyes, giving Grant a tolerant man-to-man look. "Rocks, stupid."

Elizabeth sniffed disdainfully and hunched her shoulder at her brother. "I have some rocks," she said to Grant. She straightened away from his leg and dug into the pocket of her overalls. "See?" she said, dropping a handful of small stones on the table. "This is the prettiest one." She picked up a mottled gray-blue rock and licked it. "See the colors?" She held it up for Grant's inspection.

"Very pretty," he said, wondering what her mother would say if she saw her daughter licking rocks. *Probably force the poor kid to gargle with some awful-tasting mouthwash*, he thought, remembering the way his own mother had been when it came to cleanliness and germs.

"You can have it, if you want."

The offer touched him—in unexpected places, unexpected ways. It was the first time in his memory that he'd been exposed to the spontaneous, selfless offer of a child. He didn't know what to say. "I couldn't take your prettiest rock, Lizzie," he said, surprised to find his hand lifting to caress her curly blond head. It was silky soft under his callused fingertips.

"No, it's okay. Really," she urged, her little face serious. "You can have it."

"She has lots more in her room," Sean put in. "Mom says she's a pack rat."

"You're sure you want to give it away?"

Elizabeth nodded.

"Okay." He took the rock and dropped it into his shirt pocket. "Thank you, Lizzie," he said, making a show of buttoning the pocket flap securely.

She dimpled up at him. "I can show you where I find them, if you want. I have a secret place down by the lake."

"You're not supposed to go to the lake by yourself," Sean reminded her. "You can't swim good yet."

"I can too swim! I—"

"Elizabeth! Sean!" The voice of their brother rang through the air, followed by the furious clanging of an old-fashioned dinner bell. "Dinner!"

Sean scrambled up from his chair. "Come on, Lizzie. We have to go."

Elizabeth shook her head.

"Come *on*, Lizzie." He darted a look at Grant. "Mom said we weren't supposed to bother Mr. Saxon."

"I'm not botherin' him," she said confidently, tilting her head to look up at Grant. "Am I?"

Grant smiled at her. "No, honey, you're not bothering me," he said, surprised to find that it was true. The knowledge set off all sorts of warnings in his head. He removed his hand from her hair. "But maybe you'd better go on, anyway. Sounds like your big brother's looking for you."

"Yeah, Lizzie, it's time to eat," urged Sean.

"Okay." Elizabeth straightened, taking Grant's hand in hers as she did so. "Come on," she ordered, tugging it.

"Come on where?"

"To eat."

Grant smiled. "I don't think your mother would be too pleased with that idea."

"No, it's okay," Sean assured him. "Mr. Landers and Mr. Fairfax from cabin one are coming to Sunday dinner. And Tim's gonna eat with us, too. And his girlfriend, prob'bly. Mom doesn't mind. She always says the more the merrier. She always makes lots."

Grant shook his head. "I don't think so."

"We're havin' fried chicken," Elizabeth said. "An' mashed 'tatoes an' gravy, an' corn on the cob an'—" she paused dramatically, making sure she had his full attention before she went on "—chocolate cake with 'nilla ice cream!"

Grant began to salivate; he'd been planning on nothing more elaborate than a ham sandwich and a beer for dinner.

Fried chicken, huh?

How had she known that fried chicken was the one food he couldn't resist? Dammit all, he'd bet anything that Lily Talbot made the best fried chicken in the state! It would be the kind of thing she'd do. And the chocolate cake was probably made from scratch, the ice cream probably homemade with real cream and sugar and vanilla beans. He'd be a fool to say no to a meal like that.

Knowing full well that he was only asking for trouble, Grant got up and followed the two children to the lodge.

4

"HAVE YOU TWO washed your hands?" Lily inquired, her back to the door as she heaped fluffy mounds of mashed potatoes into a pale yellow ceramic bowl with a serving spoon.

"Not yet, Mommy."

"Back into the utility room and wash," she ordered, without turning around. "Dinner will be on the table before you're finished."

"Does Mr. Saxon have to wash his hands, too?"

"Yes," Lily began automatically, not really hearing what the child had said, "Mr. Saxon has to—" she whirled around, a lump of mashed potatoes dropping from the serving spoon at her abrupt movement"—wash his hands, too," she finished weakly, her eyes widening as they settled on the man who just walked into her kitchen with her six-year-old daughter's hand in his.

He had the grace to look a little sheepish at the expression of blank astonishment on his hostess's face. "Lizzie and Sean assured me that 'the more the merrier.' I hope you don't mind."

It took Lily a minute to gather her wits enough to answer him. "Oh...oh, no, of course not. The more the merrier, certainly," she said, grabbing a dishcloth to wipe the smear of mashed potatoes that had fallen from her spoon. "I, ah . . . would have invited you myself," she lied, head bent to her task as a delicate flush of color warmed her cheeks. "But we eat so early on Sundays and I thought you'd be going into Bend for dinner later." Her shoulders lifted in an apologetic little shrug, but she didn't look up from what she was doing. "I just assumed you'd have other plans."

"I wasn't planning on anything more than a ham sandwich and a beer before these two rescued me."

Lily lifted her head, every maternal instinct she possessed recoiling at his words. "A sandwich!" she said, aghast. "That's no kind of dinner for a big, str— For someone your size," she amended quickly, sensing the suddenly interested stares of her other dinner guests. She whisked the bowl of potatoes from the tiled kitchen counter and set them on the long trestle-style table. "Jeff, set another place, please. Just move those two down a little," she instructed her elder son. "Lizzie can scoot her chair a little closer to Mr. Landers, and Mr. Saxon can sit at the end here. That way he can stretch his cast out to the side if he wants to." She looked up at Grant. "Is that all right with you?"

"That's fine." He smiled. "And the name is Grant, remember?"

Lily smiled back. "Yes, of course. Grant," she agreed, her eyes momentarily held by the look in his. *Such dark eyes to sparkle so*, she thought. For some reason, she always expected brown eyes to be more somber. More sober. But Grant Saxon's were alive with life and laughter and something else that she couldn't quite name. She looked away, shaking her head slightly as if to clear it. "Sean, you and Lizzie show Mr. Saxon where he can wash up." She fluttered her hands at them. "Go on. Dinner's already on the table."

All three of them turned obediently, Grant following the two children back out to the utility room. His tall, powerful form towered over those of Elizabeth and Sean, making him look even bigger than he was and them smaller, like a bear lumbering behind a pair of fawns—except that there was nothing bearlike about his lean hips and long jeans-clad legs. The man was shaped like a steel-shouldered wedge.

"You have to wash un'er your fingernails, too," Lily heard Elizabeth say, her high-pitched voice clear above the rush of water as she issued her orders. Grant's answer was a low rumble of sound, the words indistinguishable to Lily, but they made Sean and Elizabeth laugh.

Funny, she thought, turning back to the stove to dish up the rest of the meal. *I wouldn't have thought he'd know how to talk to children, let alone know how to make them laugh.* Yet he'd been so sweet to Lizzie earlier, she reminded herself, listening so patiently to her convoluted tale of Noah's ark, even complimenting her on her telling of it. And both Sean and Elizabeth were comfortable in his presence; they obviously felt none of the spine-tingling nervousness that affected their mother whenever Grant Saxon was in the same room.

But then, she reflected, a wry little smile curving her lips, *he probably hasn't kissed either of them.*

"Lily? Can I take that for you?" Tim's soft-voiced, raven-haired girlfriend held out her hands for the platter of fried chicken.

"Yes, thank you, Julie. Just set it at one end of the table. Tim—" she handed a second heaping platter to her handyman "—this one goes at the other end. Now—" She surveyed the laden table with an experienced eye as Grant, Sean and Elizabeth trooped back into the kitchen. "Have I forgotten anything?"

"Biscuits," said Jeff, lifting his little sister over the back of her chair as everyone took their seats.

Quickly Lily took the buttermilk biscuits out of the oven, sliding them off the hot baking sheet into a napkin-lined basket. "Watch your heads," she warned, reaching between Elizabeth and Grant to put the biscuits in a clear space on the tablecloth.

Obligingly Grant leaned back away from the table to allow her access just as she leaned forward. The back of his head nudged against her breasts. For a split second neither of them moved, both of them held stock-still by the warm, tingling sensation that raced through them. Then Grant straightened as if someone had yanked him upright with a string. Lily gasped and jerked back, dropping the basket of biscuits the last inch or two to the table. Flushing, she bustled around to her chair, being careful not to rub against or bump Grant in any way as she pulled it away from the table.

It hadn't occurred to her when she gave him the end seat that she was giving him the seat next to hers. It occurred to her now. *Darn, he's big. And so . . . so male!*

"You forgot the butter, Mom," Sean said just as she got herself settled into her chair.

"Stay there, Lily," offered Tim, jumping to his feet. "I'll get it."

"Is that *everything*?" she said, glancing down the length of the table as Tim slipped back into his seat. There was a murmur of assent. "Okay, then—" Without looking at him, she held out her hand to Grant. Her other hand was offered to Sean. "Lizzie, honey, would you like to say grace?"

Elizabeth bowed her curly blond head and recited a simple rhyme that she had learned in Sunday school, her clear, sweet voice giving it a lilting, singsong quality.

"Amen," said everyone in unison when it was over.

"Amen," Lily heard Grant say softly, half a beat after everyone else. His slight hesitation told her, more clearly than words, that he wasn't at all used to this kind of informal family gathering, with grace and children and big bowls of food meant to be passed around the table. He was probably feeling just a bit overwhelmed by it all, she thought, giving his hand a reassuring little squeeze as she prepared to pull hers away. His fingers tightened, keeping her hand where it was.

"Thank you for being so gracious about me inviting myself to dinner."

"You didn't invite yourself," she said quietly, trying very hard to ignore the warmth passing from his fingers to hers. "Sean and Elizabeth invited you."

"Without your knowledge."

"But with my full approval," she countered, meaning it. "This is their home, their table, just as much as it is mine. They're free to invite someone to Sunday dinner if they want to."

Grant smiled at her sweet seriousness. "Even a man who takes advantage of their mother?" he teased softly.

"Takes advantage?" Lily's brow wrinkled up in a frown. "I don't understand."

He leaned closer, and instinctively Lily leaned closer, too. Their foreheads were only a few inches apart. "You mean you've forgotten our kiss already?" he whispered, feigning a hurt look. "I'm crushed."

Lily's head snapped upright. "No!" The word came out in a startled squeak. She lowered her voice, her eyes darting around the table to see if anyone had heard what he said. They were all busy passing bowls and platters back and forth as they filled their plates. All except Jeff, who was watching his mother with a look that she couldn't quite decipher. Her eyes returned to Grant's. She could read *his* expression easily enough; his brown eyes sparkled with warmth and mischief.

"Does that mean you *haven't* forgotten?"

"No! I mean, yes," she said, not knowing what she meant. "That is, I—"

"Hey, Lily, you gonna pass them potatoes down this way?" called Art Fairfax from the other end of the table. "Or are ya gonna sit there holdin' hands with that good-lookin' young fella all day?" Her elderly guest's eyes were alight with pleasure at his own wit.

Lily yanked her hand out of Grant's. "We aren't holding hands."

"Sure looked like it from here." He winked at Jeff. "Didn't it look like your mother was holdin' that fella's hand to you, son?"

Jeff shrugged, his expression guarded, almost sullen, as he stared down the length of the table at his mother. "Dunno."

"Well, take my word for it. They was holdin' hands, all right. Done it a few times myself, so I know." He turned his attention back to Lily. "You gonna pass them potatoes or what?"

Her cheeks pink, Lily passed the potatoes.

"I'm sorry," Grant said to her a moment later. "I didn't mean to embarrass you in front of your guests."

"It's okay," she said without looking at him. "No harm done. Here, Sean, let me help you with that gravy before you spill it."

He waited until she'd served her son, then tried again. "Great chicken."

"Thank you." She smiled down the table at the white-haired man sitting on the other side of her daughter. Mr. Landers was the quieter of her two elderly guests and sometimes needed to be urged to help himself to seconds. "Bob, would you like some more of these green beans? They're home canned."

"Don't mind if I do, Lily. They're real tasty."

"Home canned, huh?" Grant said, helping himself to a spoonful of beans before passing them on. "I don't think I've ever had home-canned green beans before." He speared another piece of crisp golden chicken off the platter in front of him. "You raise the chickens, too?"

"No." Lily still didn't look at him. "They came from the meat case at Safeway. Lizzie, honey, don't talk with your mouth full."

"Well, it has a real melt-in-your-mouth flavor," Grant persisted. "Crisp on the outside. Tender and juicy inside."

"I'm glad you like it," she said, watching out of the corner of her eye as he bit into a plump, meaty breast.

"It's wonderful." His tongue flashed out, licking a bit of the crisp, flaky coating off his lips.

Lily redirected her gaze. "When—" She paused to clear her throat. "When are you leaving for California, Tim?"

Tim stopped playing with Julie's knee under the table. "Tuesday afternoon. And I won't be back until late Monday. Mom's having a big Thanksgiving reunion this year," he explained. "My brother's driving up from San José. My sister Beth and her husband and kids are flying in from Dallas." He smiled happily. "A dozen or so aunts and uncles and cousins coming from who knows where."

"Sounds like fun," Lily said.

Fun? Grant thought, watching her as he forked up a bite of mashed potatoes and gravy. *Obviously the poor woman doesn't know what fun is.* A small, wickedly masculine smile curved his lips. *Maybe I should give her a few lessons.* Just thinking about it made his pulse quicken.

"Me an' Sean an' Jeff are going to Daddy's house in Portlan' for Thanksgiving," offered Elizabeth. "We're gonna ride the bus!"

"No kidding?" Tim said as if he hadn't heard it a million times.

Elizabeth nodded. "Uh-huh. It takes a long time on the bus, but Daddy can't come an' get us cause Cynthia's gonna have a baby pretty soon an' she's too fat to get in the car."

"Elizabeth!" Lily admonished, trying unsuccessfully to stifle a laugh as a mental picture of her ex-husband's slim, sexy wife being too fat to get into the car formed in her mind's eye.

"Well, she is!" Elizabeth insisted. She turned in her seat, looking to Jeff for confirmation. "Isn't she, Jeff?"

Jeff shrugged and looked at his plate.

"Let's forget about Cynthia for now and just eat our dinner, shall we?" Lily said, making a mental note to have a heart-to-heart talk with her elder son before he left for his father's. His stepmother's pregnancy was obviously bothering him.

To be absolutely truthful, it was bothering her, too. Sort of. With Elizabeth growing up so fast, Lily would have loved to have another baby around to cuddle and hold. In a roundabout way, Cynthia's pregnancy had robbed her of that option. *Well, not Cynthia's pregnancy exactly*, she amended, pushing her food around on her plate. But Cynthia herself. She was the woman that Jeffrey had left Lily for.

Not that Lily begrudged her Jeffrey—the marriage had been over long before Cynthia came on the scene— but she did begrudge her the coming baby. Lily loved babies. And, considering her present circumstances, she wasn't likely to have another anytime soon. If ever.

Men willing to even *date* divorceés with three kids were as rare as hen's teeth. Never mind marriage and the prospect of more children.

"You look a little sad," Grant said softly, wondering why it bothered him so much. "Is this the first time you'll be without your kids on Thanksgiving?" *Or is it hubby's new wife and baby?*

Lily looked up, startled by his perception. Somehow that devilish sparkle in his eyes had made her think that he wasn't the perceptive type. "This isn't the first time the kids have gone to their father's for Thanksgiving," she said before she had time to consider that it wasn't really any of his business. "Jeffrey and I have been divorced for over three years and we trade off. I'll have them with me at Christmas." She sighed. "But it's always a little depressing being alone on a holiday, don't you think?"

Grant shrugged. Holidays were pretty much just another day of the year to him, celebrated casually wherever he happened to be at the time. "I don't think much about it one way or another," he said. "I'm usually off doing a story somewhere, anyway. Like now."

"Like now? You mean you're not going home for Thanksgiving?"

"Home to what?" he said, thinking of his bare-bones bachelor apartment in San Francisco. The thought wasn't very appealing, but then it never had been. It was just a place to crash between assignments.

"Don't you have a family?" she said, daring to ask the question that had been hovering on the edge of her mind ever since he'd kissed her. "A . . . a wife, or children? Parents?"

"No wife," he said, smiling a little at the way she had hesitated over the word. His having a wife would matter to a woman like Lily; she wasn't the type to enjoy having kissed a married man. "No kids, either. And my parents are both dead."

Lily's eyes clouded for a moment. "Oh, I'm so sorry." She couldn't imagine anything worse than having no family. "How terrible for you."

Grant shook his head. "Not so terrible. I've never wanted a wife. Or kids. And my parents died a long time ago. My mother when I was seventeen. My father while I was still in college. They were both in their late forties when I was born," he added, forestalling questions.

"You were an only child?" she said sympathetically. Lily had been an only child, too; that's why her children weren't.

"Yeah, my—"

"Hey, Grant." Tim spoke from across the table. "Lizzie just told me you broke your ankle rock climbing. Was it someplace around here?"

Grant shook his head. "El Capitan in Yosemite."

"Yeah?" Tim was obviously impressed. "What happened?"

"His pee-tons came out," Elizabeth said importantly. "That's what hol's you up so you don't fall down."

"Elizabeth," Lily admonished. "Let Mr. Saxon tell us about it." She glanced up at the man beside her. "Tell us what happened," she said gently, still feeling misty-eyed at his lack of family ties.

Grant shrugged. "Pete Garcia—he's a photographer—and I were about twenty-five hundred feet up the face of the cliff, and like Lizzie said—" he smiled at the little girl "—a couple of pitons pulled loose. Knocked myself silly, broke my tibia just above the ankle and dislocated my shoulder. Had to hang there like a dead fish and wait for the Park Service to come rescue me."

Lily blanched. "How terrible!"

"Yeah, but I got a hell of a story out of it." He grinned. "Even if it wasn't the one I originally went after. And Pete's pictures will probably make *Life*."

"Story?" said Tim. "You wrote a story about it? Wait a minute!" He snapped his fingers. "Are you *that* Grant Saxon? The one who writes for *National Geographic* and *Adventure* and all those sports magazines?"

Grant nodded. "The same."

"Well, I'll be . . . Hey, Lily, did you know you had a celebrity staying here?"

"No, I . . ."

"Do you really do all those things?" Julie wanted to know. "Skydiving and skiing glaciers and rafting through the Grand Canyon?"

"If I don't do it, I don't write about it."

"What's skydriving?" asked Elizabeth.

"That's sky*diving*, babycakes," Tim said, and then began to explain exactly what it was to the curious six-year-old.

Lily wasn't listening. Her thoughts were still tied up with the image of Grant Saxon dangling unconscious from the end of a rope. Unable to stop herself, unaware that she was even doing it, she looked down at the plastic-wrapped cast on his leg.

He broke that leg climbing up the side of some mountain, she thought, horrified. *And then he hung there like a...like a dead fish for who knows how long, waiting to be rescued. With a dislocated shoulder and...* She shuddered and looked away. *He might have been permanently crippled,* she thought, remembering the gruesome extent of Sean's injuries when he'd fallen from the tree. *He might even have been killed. And I would never have known him.* The thought startled her with its unexpectedness and intensity, bringing a lump of emotion to her throat.

"Hey—" the quiet voice was close to her ear "—it wasn't that bad."

"What?" Lily lifted her eyes to find Grant looking at her with a warm, amused expression in his brown eyes. "What wasn't that bad?"

"My leg. It was a simple little break. More of a stress fracture, really. This cast—" he bumped his heel against the floor "—is just for show." He grinned at her, silently inviting her to share his little joke. "Makes all the women want to take care of me."

"But you were *unconscious*."

"For about two minutes."

"You—" she gulped "—you dislocated your shoulder?"

"And it was relocated for me thirty seconds after they pulled me up."

"But weren't you scared? Weren't you absolutely terrified?"

"For a minute, maybe. While I was falling. But there isn't much time for fear at a time like that." He smiled at her, trying to tease her out of her seriousness. "I was too busy praying that one of the pitons would hold."

Lily refused to be cajoled. "But after you stopped falling?" she said, her eyes glued to his. "When you were hanging there like a . . . a dead fish?"

"After I stopped falling?" He shook his head thoughtfully. "No, I wasn't scared. Just damn pis—ah, mad at myself for doing something so stupid."

"But—"

"Hey, it happened some time ago," he said. "Nothing to worry about now."

"I . . . yes, of course." She dropped her eyes to her plate. "I'm just being silly. Jeffrey always said that I worry too much. About . . . about silly things. I'm sorry. I didn't mean to make you uncomfortable by asking so many dumb questions."

He put his hand over hers where it lay on the table. "They aren't dumb questions and you didn't make me uncomfortable. In fact, it's kind of nice having someone worry about me," he said, realizing as he spoke that he actually meant it. It *was* kind of nice having someone worry about him. He couldn't remember anyone worrying about him since his father died. "I don't think you're silly at all," he said, rubbing his fingertip over the back of her hand. "I think you're— Lily, look at me." He waited until she raised her soft blue eyes to his. "I think you're sweet, Lily," he said deliberately. "Very, very sweet."

"Mom. Hey, Mom." Sean's voice broke the fragile spell that was being woven between them. "Could me and Lizzie have our cake now? Please. Lizzie wants to build her ark."

Lily slipped her hand out from under Grant's. "Yes, of course." She stood up, pushing her chair back with the backs of her thighs. "Cake and ice cream for everyone," she said, not even noticing the disapproving way her elder son was looking at her.

5

LILY TOOK the last two sheets of pumpkin-mousse tartlets out of the oven and set them on a wire rack on the counter to cool next to the two dozen other pumpkin-mousse tartlets that she'd already baked. There were four dozen miniature loaves of spicy pumpkin bread cooling on the counter, too, and six traditional pumpkin pies with fancy crimped edges. Not to mention the five dozen pumpkin-shaped sugar cookies that she'd made for the children to take with them to their father's.

A good night's work, she thought with satisfaction, yawning as she turned off the oven. And as soon as the last dirty pan was washed and put away she'd be ready for a good night's sleep. With the kids already in bed and the house as still and quiet as a classroom on Saturday morning, she'd be asleep as soon as her head hit the pillow.

She moved over to the sink with empty baking sheets and slid them into a rubber basin of hot, soapy water. As she stood there, scrubbing them clean, her eyes wandered to the gingham-hung window. The black night outside threw her reflection back at her, the image as clear as if she had been looking into a mirror. She had changed out of her Sunday finery before dinner, but her hair was still up in its bun, untidy now, with straggling wisps and tendrils falling down over her forehead and around her ears. Her cheeks were flushed. Her eyes were uncharacteristically bright. Her mouth was soft. Soft and oddly vulnerable-looking. As if it were waiting—*yearning*—to be kissed. Again. Lily frowned at her reflection and looked away, denying what she saw.

Quickly she finished washing the baking sheets, her movements deliberately brisk as she rinsed them off under a stream of hot water and dried them with a soft terry towel before she put them away. She left the kitchen hurriedly, reaching out to flick off the light as she passed it. Then, halfway across the main room of the lodge, she turned abruptly and retraced her steps, telling herself that it was only because she'd forgotten to use the hand lotion that sat on the edge of the sink.

She reentered the kitchen, passing the light switch without turning it on, relying on the feeble glow of the moonlight coming in through the window to guide her through the familiar territory of the room. More by habit and feel than by sight she located the pump top of the lotion and dispensed a creamy pink blob into her palm. Then, as she stood there rubbing the soothing lotion into her skin, she did what she'd told herself she wouldn't do: she looked out the window again.

It was an eerily beautiful night, the kind of night that cried out to be shared with a special someone, snug inside in front of a dying fire. A strong, steady wind rustled through the pine trees, causing them to shimmer and sway to some music only they could hear. Black rain clouds rolled across the night sky, playing hide-and-seek with the flickering stars. A pale slice of moon cast its gentle, ghostly glow over the yard, gleaming off the ice-frosted puddles that hadn't soaked into the ground. But it wasn't the beauty of the night that held her attention; it was the warm yellow light spilling from the front window of cabin four that drew her eyes like a beacon.

Grant Saxon sat in that pool of light, his well-shaped head bent over the typewriter on the desk in front of him, his blunt-tipped fingers tapping out what must have been a staccato rhythm on the keys. Every so often he paused in his typing, rummaging through the papers and brochures piled beside the typewriter as if to verify a fact, skimming over the copy he had just written, picking up a stubby pencil to make a correction. Even just sitting there, Lily thought, doing nothing more physical than typing, he looked full of life and vitality, ready at any minute to burst up from his chair.

Suddenly, as if her thought had somehow provoked him to action, he did shoot up from his chair. With a silent curse that Lily could read even from across the width of the yard, he ripped the paper out of his typewriter, balled it up in his fist and threw it in the direction of the fireplace. Then he turned toward the window, looked directly at the lodge and glared.

Lily froze, thinking for one panicked moment that he was glaring at her. But then she realized that he couldn't be; the lodge was dark and silent; there was no way he could see her standing here in the kitchen. He wasn't really looking at anything, anyway, she told herself. He was merely looking out into the darkness, his thoughts focused inward on the article that was apparently giving him trouble. That's what he was frowning at so ferociously. Not her. He didn't even know she was there.

But, oh, how I wish he did. The thought came out of nowhere, surprising her with its wistfulness and longing.

"Lily Talbot, you're crazy," she said aloud. "And you'd better get yourself to bed before you do something that proves it."

But she didn't move from the window. She stood there staring at Grant Saxon's handsome, mobile face, watching his glare turn to a rueful twist of his lips as he sank into the straight-backed chair in front of the desk and rolled another piece of paper into the typewriter.

He resumed tapping on the keys, his left hand automatically lifting to operate the carriage-return lever at the end of each line. On the fifth line he hesitated and paused, and his hand lifted to the back of his neck instead. He rotated his head from side to side, as if easing an ache, and then, slowly, he turned and looked at the darkened lodge again. His expression conveyed a myriad of conflicting emotions—desire, indecision, denial, resolve—all in such quick succession that Lily wasn't sure she had really seen any of them. Then he shook his head, his broad shoulders lifting in a deep sigh, and turned back to the typewriter.

He's working too hard, Lily thought, compassion flooding her. *He's pushing himself to do too much after that awful accident. He needs someone to make him take things a little slower. Someone to rub his neck for him and—* She pulled herself up sharply. No, she couldn't rub his neck for him. That would be asking for trouble, she thought, unconsciously licking her lips as she remembered the way he had kissed her the other morning without the slightest provocation on her part. Undoubtedly he would misinterpret any offer to massage the tension out of his neck as a sexual advance of some kind.

Well, wasn't it?

No, she told herself firmly, shaking her head as if someone else had posed the question. No, she meant nothing sexual by it at all. She simply wanted to offer a fellow human being a little comfort, a little . . .

Pumpkin bread, she thought, her eyes falling on the loaves cooling on the kitchen counter. She could take him some fresh-baked pumpkin bread to go with the cup of coffee that was sitting by his elbow. He'd at least have to stop working long enough to eat it.

Without giving herself time to question her real motives, Lily pulled a small wicker tray from the cupboard next to the refrigerator. Draping it with a pale yellow napkin, she quickly arranged a miniature loaf of pumpkin bread atop it, added a small crock of sweet butter, another of golden honey and, as a final touch, half a dozen of the sugar cookies that she'd made for her kids.

I'll just take this over to him, she told herself, nudging the screen door open with her hip, *and then I'll leave. I won't even go in.* She hurried across the yard, hunching her shoulders against the hint of coming snow that chilled the night air, and knocked softly on the door of cabin four.

The typewriter keys fell silent.

Lily knocked again, carefully balancing the tray against one hip with her other hand.

"Who is it?"

"It's me," she said hesitantly. "Lily Talbot. I've brought you some—"

The door swung back on its hinges as if it had been blown open by a hurricane.

"—thing to eat," she finished, slightly breathless. "I thought you might like a little snack."

Grant pushed the screen door open. "Come in. Come in." His hand closed around her upper arm. "You must be freezing out there."

"No, I can't. Really," she said firmly, allowing him to usher her inside. "I just wanted to drop this by before I went to, ah...bed," she finished in a mumble, her eyes drawn to the queen-size on the opposite wall of the small, cozy cabin. Firelight flickered over the rumpled sheets, giving the white percale a golden glow. Both pillows were propped against the headboard invitingly. The thick plaid bedspread lay in a tangled heap on the floor. *It's only an unmade bed*, she told herself, looking away from it. *Nothing you haven't seen before. So just give him the tray and go.* "I thought you might be hungry."

"Starving," he assured her. "Here, let me take that for you." He took the laden tray from her hands, setting it on the table, and pulled out a chair. "Sit down. Make yourself comfortable. Would you like some coffee?"

"No, really. I can't." She followed him into the kitchen area with cautious steps, pausing just behind the chair he'd pulled out for her. "I just wanted to drop off the pumpkin bread and get right back. The children . . ." she said vaguely, thinking, *Yes, the children. What would they think if they knew their mother was in a man's cabin, alone, at eleven o'clock at night, with an unmade bed not ten feet away?*

"Just one cup?" he coaxed, his hand already lifting the pot from the counter. He turned to smile at her over his shoulder. "I made it fresh a little while ago."

All thoughts of the children disappeared from Lily's mind. She sank into the chair. "Well, okay—just one."

"Wonderful." He grabbed a thick ceramic mug off a hook under the cabinet. "Milk? Sugar?"

"Lots of milk," she said faintly, wondering if she was crazy to be sitting here. *Yes!* "No sugar."

"Here you go." He slid the mug onto the table under her nose and sat down in the ladder-back chair opposite, twisting it around first so that he could straddle it. He folded his arms across the top rung. "Hope it's the way you like it."

Lily picked up the coffee and sipped it. "Yes, it's fine." She smiled shyly at him over the rim, not quite daring to meet his eyes. "Perfect."

He smiled back at her, his white teeth flashing in his rugged face, the tiny laugh lines at the corners of his eyes crinkling into the chestnut hair at his temples. "I'm glad. I was afraid it might be too strong for you."

"It couldn't be bet—" Her eyes met his.

Wide blue eyes stared into reckless brown for a few endless seconds. For an instant, a heartbeat only, communication flashed between them—interest, attraction, need, heat. Such heat. It sizzled, unspoken, on the air between them.

Lily reddened and looked down into her coffee cup.

Grant cleared his throat, shifting surreptitiously in his chair to ease the sudden restriction of his jeans. "So," he said, casting around in his mind for an innocent, innocuous topic of conversation. Because if one of them didn't say something he was going to jump her. He was going to grab her out of that chair and lay her down on the kitchen table and— His glance fell on the tray between them. "So," he said again, licking his lips to moisten them. "What goodies have you brought me?"

Lily started guiltily, her eyes flashing to his face for a startled moment. "G-goodies?"

Grant flicked a hand toward the tray, missing her revealing expression because his own eyes were lowered. "The bread. What kind is it?"

"Oh. Oh, *goodies*." She seized the topic gratefully, wondering if he had any idea what she thought he'd meant; hoping fervently that he hadn't. "It's, um, pumpkin bread," she said without looking at him. "It should be still warm." She touched it lightly with two fingers. "Yes, still warm. And this is sweet butter, and honey. I get it locally. The honey, that is. There's a farmer—Bill Halsey—just outside Sisters who keeps a few hives and he sells the honey to make a little extra income. It's very good." She was rambling, she knew, but she couldn't seem to help it. She always rambled when she was nervous. "And these are sugar cookies. The kids love them."

"You made all this for me?" His voice was gently teasing, but Lily didn't hear the bantering note.

"Well, not *for* you, exactly," she said honestly, daring to peek at him from under her lashes. He was staring at her with the most avid expression on his face, as if he were ten years old and she were a sugar cookie. She looked away quickly. "I was baking for my restaurant account and watching you—" She flushed and bit her lip. "That is, I happened to glance out the window and saw you working and I thought you might like a bedti— ah, midnight snack," she corrected herself, feeling the heat in her cheeks intensify. That was the second time she'd stumbled over the word *bed. He's going to think I'm a poor sex-starved divorcée throwing out desperate lures. Just like the other morning.* The legs of her chair screeched against the wooden floor as she got to her feet. "Well, I guess I'd better go." Her voice was breathless. She felt hot all over. "I've kept you from your work long enough."

Grant stood, too, barely restraining himself from reaching out for her. She was so lovely, standing there all flustered and pink cheeked with embarrassment. So incredibly sweet and naive to even *be* embarrassed. And so damned sexy that she was burning a hole in his gut. "You haven't kept me from my work."

"But..." She motioned limply toward the type-writer.

"I wasn't working, believe me." *I was thinking about you. About undressing you, slowly, in that bed in front of the fire.* He smiled crookedly, indicating the balled papers that littered the floor around the desk with a tilt of his head. "Does that look to you as if I was getting any work done?"

"Then I really *should* go," Lily said firmly, trying to convince herself as much as she was him. "You need to get some work done, and I'm keeping you from it."

Grant shook his head. "I've done all I'm going to do tonight. For the past hour it's just been busywork, anyway, because I didn't have anything else to do. There's no TV in here," he explained before she could ask. "I don't feel like reading anymore about the recreational facilities of Bend. And I'm not ready for bed yet." *At least not to sleep!* "I'd really like you to stay for a while, Lily. I could use someone to talk to besides myself," he said, appealing directly to her soft heart. He smiled cajolingly. "Please."

Lily felt herself weakening under the onslaught of that smile, that plea. Half of her wanted desperately to stay and have him smile at her again; the other half was urging her to run like hell.

"At least finish your coffee before you go."

Her desperate half won. What harm was there in sharing a cup of coffee and a little conversation with him? "All right." She reseated herself. "But just this one cup. And then I really have to go."

"Great! Just let me get myself a refill and I'll join you." He turned toward the desk to get his coffee mug. *You're acting like a horny kid, Saxon,* he warned himself, trying to suppress his body's response to her capitulation. *Cool it.* "We can have—" *Each other,* his body clamored. He ignored it. "—A couple of slices of that pumpkin bread."

"I loathe pumpkin," Lily said, and then, "Good Lord, Grant, your leg!"

Grant stopped and looked down at his legs. They both looked perfectly normal to him; a matched pair in worn jeans and heavy gray sweatsocks. "What about it?"

"Your cast is gone!"

"Oh, that." He shrugged. "I took it off after dinner."

"Took it off! But why? How?"

"With a hacksaw that I borrowed from Tim."

"With a hacksaw... Are you crazy?" She half turned in her chair, her eyes following him as he carried his cup to the kitchen counter and refilled it. "You could have done irreparable damage to your leg by taking that cast off too soon."

"Naw." He straddled his chair and took a quick swallow of coffee. "It was ready to come off."

"Then you should have gone to your doctor and let him do it." As far as Lily was concerned, all injuries should be treated by a doctor. Preferably by a team of doctors. Specialists. "You do have a doctor, don't you?" she asked suspiciously.

"My doctor is in San Francisco. Besides, there was no need. I've done it before. Nothing to it."

"Done it before?" Lily's eyes widened. "You mean this isn't the first time you've broken your leg?"

Grant shook his head. "Fourth," he said, grinning at the horrified look on her face.

"Fourth! You've broken your leg *four* times? Good Lord, how?"

"The first time was in high school. This big defensive tackle sat on my ankle. Snapped it right in two." A reminiscent smile touched his lips. "You could hear the bone crack from one end of the stadium to the other."

Lily put a hand to her throat.

"The second time was a skydiving accident. But that was the other leg." He got up from the table again and opened a drawer at the kitchen counter. "I landed wrong and ended up with a compound fracture of the right fibula. It was my first jump and—"

Lily turned away and covered her ears. "I don't want to hear it." A compound fracture was what Sean had had; there had been blood everywhere.

"The third time was just a simple hairline fracture like this one." He swung his leg over the chair and sat down. "Nothing serious."

"Nothing serious!" She lowered her hands and stared at him across the tiny table. "You are crazy. A broken leg is extremely serious. You could have been crippled for life or left with a limp or—"

"Here." He slid a knife, handle end forward, toward her. "Why don't you slice us a piece of that pumpkin bread before it gets cold?"

She stared at him for a moment, unable to make the switch from broken bones to pumpkin bread.

He smiled at her perplexity. "On second thought, I'd better do it." He pulled the knife back across the table. "You're so worked up you might cut yourself." His eyes twinkled at her. "And I know what a coward you are about blood."

"I am not worked up," she said, shaking her head at the offered slice of pumpkin bread.

"You sure?" he asked, meaning the bread. "It looks delicious."

"And I'm not a coward," she added, ignoring his comment about the bread. "I'm just—" she paused, searching for the right words "—cautious and sensible."

"You're a lily-livered, jelly-spined coward," he said, digging the tip of the knife into the butter. "One tiny little drop of blood and you turn green." He smeared the butter on his slice of pumpkin bread.

"Please." She shuddered delicately and reached for a sugar cookie. "Not while I'm eating."

"Not while you're eating, my as—eye." He grinned at her, the knife in his hand held poised over the crock of honey. "Not anytime."

"Okay, not anytime," she agreed. "Blood is not my favorite topic of discussion," she added, feeling suddenly, inexplicably, very much at ease with this man. Still aware of him in a purely feminine way, of course, but comfortable. Jeffrey had always made her feel slightly ashamed of her squeamishness; she hadn't been able to assist him in his dental practice because of it. Grant made her feel as if it were merely an amusing quirk in her personality.

"Here, give me that." She put her untasted cookie down. "You'll only make a mess doing it that way," she admonished, taking the knife from him to scrape it against the side of the crock of honey. "You need a butter knife or a spoon. No, stay there, I'll get it." She jumped up from the table and got a teaspoon.

"Hold the bread a little closer, right over the crock," she ordered, not stopping to think that he was probably old enough to manage it on his own. "Here, let me." She reached out to take the slice of bread from him at the same time that he moved it closer. Honey dribbled from the spoon, golden droplets of the sticky stuff trickling through the fine hairs on the back of his hand. "Oh, dear. I'm sorry." Lily swiped at the oozing goo with her fingertips, trying to catch it before it dripped onto the table. "I accuse you of making a mess, then I make one myself."

"It was my fault. I wasn't holding it close enough."

"No, I take full responsibility," she said, lifting her sticky fingers to her mouth. "I should've let you do it your—" The words stuck in her throat as Grant reached out and took her wrist in his hand.

"Allow me," he said, bringing her fingers to his own lips. His tongue snaked out and licked the tip of her index finger. "Ummm, delicious," he said in a low tone, and licked it again.

For a moment Lily just stood there, still as a stone, and stared. He was licking her finger. No . . . no, now he was— Good Lord, now he was sucking on her finger! Lily gasped and jerked her hand away. The teaspoon rattled against the table. "I'll get you something to clean up with," she said, heat flooding her as she turned away. Blindly she yanked a paper towel off the roll and stuck it under the water faucet. It took her a second to remember that she had to turn on the water if she wanted it wet. She reached out, fumbling for the handle.

No one had ever done that to her before—caressed her so casually yet in such a blatantly sexual way. No one. Not even Jeffrey during their twelve years of marriage. She was utterly amazed at the wave of desire that had surged through her when Grant's tongue touched her fingertip. Desire that was still surging through her. *Maybe I am a sex-starved divorcée*, she thought frantically. *Maybe three years is too long, even for me. Maybe—*

Grant's hand covered hers on the spigot, turning it off, then traveled slowly up her arm to her shoulder. His other hand cupped her opposite shoulder. He kneaded her softly through the fabric of her sweater.

She shuddered, a thousand tiny currents of feeling darting through her at his caress, and dropped the wet paper towel.

His mouth touched her ear, his breath warm and feather soft against her skin. "Lily?" he whispered, his hands on her shoulders, silently urging her to turn to him.

She tensed, biting her lip in an agony of longing and desire, and closed her eyes. Her hands gripped the edge of the sink.

Grant hesitated, suddenly unsure. His kneading fingers stilled their caress. Was she telling him yes or no? Was her trembling silence urging him to go on or pleading with him to stop? For the first time in his adult

life he didn't know. Not for sure. And he had to know
before he could take this a step further.

"I thought you wanted me to...to, ah..." Damn! Was
there any way to say it except to say it? He'd thought
she wanted him to come on to her. No, dammit, he
knew she wanted him to come on to her. But he also
knew that she didn't want to want it. And she was right.
Hadn't he already told himself that he wasn't going to
get involved with her? They were totally, completely
wrong for each other.

Besides, ambivalent emotion had never appealed to
him; he wanted honest, eager passion or nothing. He
dropped his hands and stepped back. "I misread your
signals. I'm sorry. It won't happen again."

Lily whirled around. "No! I mean— That is—" She
took a deep breath, blushing furiously, and looked up
into his eyes. Her heart was beating so hard that she
could feel it pounding in her fingertips. "You didn't
misread any signals, Grant."

He stared down at her for a moment, trying to remember all the reasons he had just given himself for not
kissing her. But it was no use. He *wanted* to kiss her. He
had never, in his whole life, wanted to kiss anyone as
much as he wanted to kiss Lily Talbot right then. He put
his hands on her shoulders again, lifting her into him
as he bent his head. "Temptress," he said, just before his
mouth took hers.

There was nothing ambivalent about the kiss—for
either of them. Grant was all aroused masculine
aggression; Lily was feminine submission incarnate.
His tongue probed the soft barrier of her lips, demand-

ing entrance. She gave it willingly. His arms enfolded her, demanding unresisting compliance to his embrace. She melted against him, boneless and wanting. His palm cupped her breast, the soft stroke of his thumb demanding complete surrender, and she gave him that, too, because she could do nothing less. She wanted to do nothing less.

Feeling her wholehearted surrender, Grant relaxed. He took the time to explore her mouth thoroughly, almost leisurely, able to hold himself in check now that his initial claim had been made and accepted. He trailed his lips across her face, tasting the sweetness of her flushed cheeks and rounded chin and the tender flesh at the curve of her jaw. She moaned softly and let her head fall back. "Sweet, sweet temptress," he murmured, brushing his mouth against the soft bared skin of her throat. "I *ache* for you."

He bent then, without another thought for all the reasons he shouldn't, and lifted her effortlessly into his arms. It only took six steps for him to cross the room. She felt the mattress give beneath their combined weight as he lowered her to the bed, felt the messy, rumpled sheets under her back, and thought fleetingly that they would be more comfortable if they smoothed them first. Then his lips touched her breast through the fabric of her sweater, his arms gathering her close as he settled beside her, and the fleeting thought was gone.

"I've wanted to do this since that first night in your kitchen," he murmured, nuzzling to find her nipple with his mouth. "When you were standing there in your nightgown drying my hair, I wanted to do this." His lips opened over her, his breath hot and moist against her yearning flesh. "I wondered what you would taste like."

Pleasure seared through her. Pleasure at both his words and his actions. "D-did you?"

"Oh, yes. I did. I do. And now I'm going to find out." His hand slipped up under her sweater, slid up over the smooth, quivering skin of her stomach. "I'll bet you're sweet," he said softly, his eager fingers tracing the lacy edge of her bra. He found the front clasp and un-hooked it. "Sweeter than that honey you brought me. And soft." He pushed the fabric up, out of his way, and brushed her nipple with his lips.

They both sighed.

"I was right," he breathed against her. "Sweeter than honey." He transferred his attention to her other breast, rubbing his cheek against her distended nipple before taking it into his mouth. "Soft as a feather bed."

Lily sighed again, the sound turning into a moan of feminine need as his tongue continued to tease her. She put her hands on either side of his head. "Grant. Oh, Grant."

He lifted his head to look at her. His eyes, those reckless, laughing eyes, were nearly black with passion. "Too much?" he questioned softly, searching her face. "Not enough?"

Yes, she thought. It was too much and not enough. Too much because she shouldn't have been there with him at all. Not enough because she wanted, at that moment, to be with him forever. Impossible questions. "Yes," she said aloud, answering them both. "Yes."

He slid up her body and took her mouth again, thrusting his tongue between her lips the way he longed to thrust himself into her body. His hand moved down to the snap on her jeans and tugged it open.

Lily stiffened, suddenly shocked at the realization of what was happening. Of what she was letting happen. How had they gotten here so fast? From a casual caress to almost total abandon in such a short time? Minutes only, she marveled. It had taken just minutes for her to forget . . . everything. Herself. The children. The fact that the man holding her in his arms was a virtual stranger.

She tore her mouth away from his. "Grant . . . Grant, stop." She panted breathlessly.

He didn't seem—or didn't want—to hear her. "God, you're sweet," he murmured, his fingers burrowing under the elastic edge of her panties.

She grabbed his hand. "Grant, stop." There was an edge of panic to her voice. "Please."

He went very still against her. "Why?"

"Because I . . . because . . ." *Because I've changed my mind?* There was a not-very-nice word for women who did that at this late stage of the game. But this wasn't a game, not for her, and she *had* changed her mind.

"You want me." Grant's voice was low and ragged. "I want you. Why?" he repeated.

"Because I . . . I'm not protected," she said desperately, grabbing at the only excuse she could think of that might make sense to him, realizing as she said it that it was true. *And I get pregnant at the drop of a hat.* The thought sent a strange thrill through her, but she didn't have time to examine the feeling. "I haven't been on the, um, the Pill since my divorce."

Some of the tension went out of Grant's body at her words. Not on the Pill since her divorce. He liked the implication of that statement. "Don't worry." He kissed her neck reassuringly, tenderly, and levered himself up on an elbow. "I'll take care of it," he said, brushing back the tousled hair on her forehead.

"No . . . no, you don't understand." She swallowed. "I can't."

His hand stilled on her face. "Can't?" He pushed himself to a more upright position and stared down at her, unable to believe what he had just heard. *"Can't?"*

She looked away, unable to meet the accusation in his eyes. If he murdered her now it would be no more than she deserved. "I know. I know. And I'm sorry. I shouldn't have . . . have led you on . . . B-but I wasn't thinking, I was just—" The words tumbled out, breathy and disjointed, as she struggled to right her clothing. "I'm sorry," she said again, meaning it with all her heart. "But it happened s-so fast and I hardly know you and . . . and one of the children might wake up and . . ."

"One of the children? What in hell do your children have to do with this?" The acrimonious question was purely rhetorical, a way to vent his frustration. He knew what her children had to do with it: everything.

Her children were the main reason that neither of them should be doing what they were doing; they were tangible proof that their mother and Grant Saxon were different kinds of people. She was a woman with responsibilities and a lifelong commitment. He was a man who wanted neither of those things.

The blood that had begun to cool at her first words of explanation plummeted to freezing. He pushed himself off the bed and got to his feet. "Here, let me help you up."

Lily eyed his extended hand warily. "You're not mad?" she said in a small voice.

"Mad?" He looked down at her, lying there on the bed with her clothes barely pulled together and her mouth swollen from his kisses. "No, I'm not mad." He hauled her to her feet, gritting his teeth as the sweet fragrance of her hair assailed him. "Disappointed," he said ruefully, "but not mad." He released her hand and stepped back, out of temptation's way. "You were absolutely right to call a halt. Absolutely," he repeated, almost to himself. "I shouldn't have started it."

"No, you shouldn't—" She stopped, her own sense of fair play demanding honesty at least. "You didn't start it, Grant. I did. I'm the one who came to your cabin, not the other way around."

"To bring me a snack," he said, defending her.

She shook her head, determined to make a clean breast of it. "No, I came over here to . . . to—"

"To bring me some of your fresh-baked pumpkin bread," he said firmly, not wanting to hear her say what she had really come to his cabin for. Hell, he knew what she had come for as well as she did. But if she put it into words he might just be tempted to start where they had just left off. And neither of them needed that. "And I appreciate it but—" he motioned toward the desk "—I really should get back to work now," he said, disregarding the fact that he'd already told her that he hadn't been doing any work.

"Yes. Yes, of course." Gratefully Lily allowed him his polite fiction. "I shouldn't have bothered you while you were working." She sidled toward the door as she spoke. "Well, ah . . ." Her eyes lifted to his for a fleeting second. "Good night, Grant," she said softly.

"Good night, Lily."

Slowly, carefully, she pulled the door closed behind her. And then she ran across the yard to the lodge as if all the hounds of hell were snapping at her heels instead of just the temptation to turn around and run back into his arms.

6

THEY MANAGED, somehow, to stay away from each other for almost two whole days. Against every inclination of his night-owl soul Grant was up and away from the Talbot Family Resort before Lily's kids left for school, and he was careful not to come back until after dinner.

He spent those two days doggedly investigating the recreational facilities in and around Bend. He interviewed owners of companies who organized whitewater rafting trips on the Deschutes River and was informed that the best time for the wildest ride was just after the spring runoff began. He spoke to camping outfitters at Elk Lake who ran pack trains into the Three Sisters Wilderness and found out that Oregon-bred llamas were slowly gaining favor as the pack animals of choice among some wilderness guides. He visited the Mount Bachelor ski area and heard all about the newest, longest lift that made the uppermost slopes of the mountain accessible. He spoke to cross-country skiers who extolled the virtues of the area's nearly three hundred miles of marked trails, naturalists who filled him in on the glories of the Crane Prairie Reservoir where bald eagles and osprey nested, Oregon cowboys who regaled him with tales of the summer rodeo season and avid anglers who were more than happy to argue about the best lake for catching sockeye salmon and "redsides."

For two whole days he was busy and occupied—and very nearly bored out of his skull.

It would have been different, he thought irritably, if he could have actually participated in some of the activities he was researching. But he couldn't raft the Deschutes because the season was considered over in September. He couldn't ski Mount Bachelor or try out the miles of cross-country trails because the snowfall had been considerably below normal for the year so far—and his ankle probably wasn't up to it even if the snow had been perfect. Backpacking into the wilderness, on his own or with a train, took a lot of advance preparation, which he hadn't done. As for fishing . . . Hell, you had to get up too damned early to outguess a wily, temperamental steelhead. And he had never had the patience for fishing, anyway.

So he listened and took pages of notes and thought about the taste of Lily Talbot's rose-tipped breasts.

It wasn't that he wanted to think about her, dammit. He just couldn't seem to avoid it; people wouldn't let him stop thinking about her.

"Man, the rush of adrenaline you get when the raft plunges into that mother of a Souse Hole is incredible. No feeling on earth can match it!" enthused a young rafting guide.

Except holding Lily in your arms, Grant thought, scribbling nonsense onto the notepad in front of him.

"Everything's so serene and quiet with just the wind sighing through the trees," offered a cross-country skier as she launched into a lengthy explanation as to why it was her favorite sport.

Lily sighed when I kissed her, Grant thought, drifting off as he remembered the sweet, breathy sound she had made when he'd touched her breast for the first time. His notes became doodles.

"The flesh is so firm and sweet tasting," said a fisherman, explaining his preference for coho salmon over the stronger-tasting chinook.

Grant's pencil point broke against his notepad. *"What?"* he burst out, afraid for a moment that the man had been reading his mind.

"Well, I know some people feel different, o' course, but in my opinion coho is a better-tasting fish," the angler said, refusing to change his opinion even in the face of Grant's furious scowl. "Not that chinook isn't just fine for them that likes it," he added placatingly.

Grant decided it was time he called it a day. It was late, anyway. He was tired. And his ankle was even beginning to ache a little. Besides, by the time he made the drive back to the lodge, Lily and the kids would be safe inside, just starting their dinner, and he would be safe from temptation.

Only they weren't and he wasn't.

Lily and the three children were just coming out of the lodge when Grant pulled into the yard and parked in front of his cabin. She was wearing her gray sweater dress again, he noted, with high black boots this time and a fuzzy, fringed shawl that snuggled around her shoulders like a warm hug. Her hair was twisted up on the back of her head, showing off the tender nape of her neck and the firm line of her jaw. She was wearing pink lipstick and little silver button earrings. Grant had only to close his eyes to remember the faint, sweet scent of her perfume. All vestiges of the long day left him at the sight of her.

"Hello," he said, calling out a greeting before he could tell himself not to. "Where're you all headed off to?"

Lily looked up at the sound of his voice, unable to stop herself. She'd heard his Jeep pull up, of course, but she'd forced herself not to look. She knew what would happen if she looked at him. Exactly what *was* happening. *Oh, Lord,* she thought, feeling her heart start to flutter at the sight of him.

"Mr. Saxon!" Elizabeth shouted excitedly before anyone else could say a word. "Mr. Saxon, look at me! I'm an *Indian*!" She broke away from the family group and went dashing across the yard before her mother could stop her. "I'm an Indian," she repeated, twirling in front of him so that the long fringe on her dress flared out around her. "Don't I look good?"

Reluctantly Grant tore his eyes away from Lily to look at her daughter. What he saw brought a smile to his face. Lizzie's bright blue eyes and fair skin were framed by a black yarn wig. Held in place by a beaded headband, it had long pigtails that reached nearly to her waist. Her homemade "Indian" dress fell straight from her shoulders to midcalf and was decorated with long fringe at the hem and sleeves and simple bead embroidery across the bodice. She wore leather moccasins on her feet and carried a large wicker basket filled with dried ears of colorful Indian corn.

"You look beautiful," he said, meaning it. "Are you going to a costume party?"

"No! I *tol'* you—" She reached up and grabbed his hand with no more self-consciousness than a gamboling puppy grabbing hold of a stick. "I'm an Indian! In the Thanksgiving Pageant!" She danced around, drawing him across the yard before he quite knew what had happened. "I get to give the corn to the Pilgrims. On the stage," she said importantly, casting a disparaging glance at her brothers out of the corners of her eyes. "Sean only gets to sit on the chairs in front of the stage."

"I'm in the orchestra," Sean corrected, holding up his trumpet case as if to prove it.

"An' Jeff doesn't get to do nothing at all," Elizabeth went on as if Sean hadn't spoken. "He has to sit in the audience with Mommy." She looked up at Grant with a cajoling little smile. "You can sit in the audience, too, if you want," she invited, as if she hadn't just dismissed that very activity as unimportant.

"Elizabeth!" Too late, Lily tried to curb her daughter's impulsive tongue. She reached out and put a restraining hand on the child's shoulder. "I know you're excited about your first pageant, honey, but not everyone else is."

"But he can come, anyway, can't he, Mommy?" Elizabeth the irrepressible said, twisting around to look up at her mother. "Tim already went to California for Thanksgiving."

"Yeah, Mom," put in Sean, completely unaware of the undercurrents between the two adults. "Mr. Saxon could have Tim's seat." There had been no tickets purchased for the pageant, but seats had been reserved so the PTA would have an idea of how much punch and cookies to provide after the performance. One had been reserved for Tim before it was known that he wouldn't be able to attend.

"I don't think *he* wants to sit and watch a bunch of little kids he's not even related to put on a stupid Thanksgiving play," Jeff said, glaring a warning at his younger brother and sister. His tender young mouth almost achieved a sneer as he looked at Grant, all but daring him to disagree.

Don't worry, kid, Grant thought, wondering why the teenager was so hostile to him. *I don't want to go any more than you want me to.*

"Yes, he does want to!" Elizabeth said then. She looked up at Grant for confirmation. "Don't you?"

"Well, I—" *Hell, no, I don't want to*, he thought again. Sitting through a grade school pageant didn't sound like his idea of a fun way to spend an evening. And even if it was, how could he trust himself not to take the opportunity to make another pass at Lily? Even right now, with her kids surrounding them, he found himself remembering how she had looked tumbled beneath him on the bed with the firelight turning her skin to a rosy gold. It played hell with his self-control.

"Don't you want to come an' watch me?" Lizzie's bottom lip held the suspicion of a quiver.

Damn! What could he say with her looking up at him like that? How could he deny the child anything with those innocent blue eyes turned up to him so trustingly?

"Elizabeth, you're putting Mr. Saxon on the spot," Lily admonished, knowing full well that her daughter's invitation stemmed mainly from a desire to have one more pair of hands to applaud her performance. "I'm sure he has other plans for tonight."

"Well, no, I don't," he began automatically. Too late, he saw his mistake. "That is—"

"See, I *tol'* you he wanted to come," Elizabeth squealed triumphantly. "He can come, can't he, Mommy?" she pleaded, as if Grant were a playmate her own age.

"Elizabeth," Lily said in exasperation, wondering if it was too late to put a gag on her tactless child. It would be best, she knew, if he didn't come to the pageant with them. But it would be rude to say so, now that it had been established that he had no other plans for the evening. Lily stifled a sigh, staunchly ignoring the tremor of excitement that raced along her nerve endings at the thought of having him sit next to her in a darkened auditorium.

"Yes, of course, Lizzie," she said briskly, trying to pretend that it didn't matter to her one way or the other. "If Mr. Saxon wants to come, he'd be very welcome." She lifted her eyes to Grant's for the first time in two long days and issued the invitation directly. "We'd be happy to have you come with us," she said, wondering how she was going to survive an entire evening in his company—under her children's chaperonage, no less!—when all she had to do was look at him to feel again what she had felt in his arms.

"I'd love to come with you," he said, the look in his eyes inadvertently giving the words a far different meaning than the one he had intended.

Lily's mouth formed an astonished little moue.

"I mean, ah . . ." *Dammit, Saxon, straighten up your act!* "Yes, I'd like to go to the pageant with you." He looked down at Elizabeth with a crooked little smile, trying to make it seem as if it were her invitation he were accepting. "Wouldn't want to miss the star's debut performance, would I?"

"She's not the star," Sean jeered. "She doesn't even get to say anything."

Elizabeth rounded on her brother. "I do, too!"

"Do not."

"Do—"

"That's enough, both of you." Lily pulled Elizabeth back before she could slug her brother. "Lizzie, I'm sure Mr. Saxon will be sorry he said yes if you continue to act like a little hooligan."

The child subsided instantly.

"That's better. Now, in the car, all of you, before we're late. Go on." She shooed them toward the car ahead of her.

Grant put his hand on Lily's arm, detaining her as she moved to follow the children. "You don't think I need to change?"

"In the back seat, Jeff. Between Lizzie and Sean, please," she said, before turning to look at Grant, trying

to act as if her arm weren't tingling beneath his touch.
"I'm sorry." Her voice held a touch of unintentional
hauteur. "What did you say?"

He dropped his hand. "Do I need to change?"

Her eyes ran over him quickly, trying to look at his
clothes without seeing anything else. He wore sturdy
hiking boots, laced tightly to the ankle, clean well-worn
jeans that hugged his long legs and narrow hips, a tan-
and-blue plaid shirt that lay smoothly over his broad
chest and a tan corduroy sport jacket that fell loosely
from his wide shoulders without doing anything to hide
the muscular torso beneath it.

"You look fine," she said in a strained voice. *More
than fine. Fantastic. You smell fantastic, too,* she
thought, unconsciously leaning closer to breathe in the
scent of fresh air and man and the lingering hint of a
faintly musky after-shave.

"You don't think I need a tie?" he asked softly, drinking in the intoxicating wildflower fragrance that surrounded her.

"A tie?" Her gaze moved to his bared throat. "No,
you don't need a tie." It would be a shame to cover that
strong brown throat with a tie, to hide that intriguing
wedge of crisp dark hair exposed by his open collar.
"Sean's only wearing one because he's in the orchestra."

"You're sure?" His voice was barely above a whisper
and he stood very still, like a man on the verge of lur-
ing a wild bird to light on his hand. Another step and
she'd be in his arms.

"Bend's not a fancy-dress town," she murmured, moving closer. Only a tiny half step but, still, closer. "You must have noticed."

"Yes, I—"

A car horn blared and they jumped apart like guilty children, both of them looking toward the source of the noise.

Two of the car's passengers were leaning over the front seat, but it was impossible to tell whether Jeff had honked the horn, or whether he was reaching out to stop his little sister from doing it.

"Come *on*, Mommy!" Lizzie hollered. "We're gonna be late for my day-butte."

TO HIS ASTONISHMENT Grant enjoyed the Thanksgiving Pageant. He enjoyed it very much. Entering the crowded auditorium with Lily and her children had been the first surprise. He had expected to feel different somehow. A breed apart. The confirmed bachelor among the dedicated parents of the world. But no one stared to see him in such an unlikely place. No one even seemed to pay him any particular attention beyond a few speculative glances as Lily introduced him around in the few minutes they had before the performance started. It gave him a peculiar sense of belonging to be so easily accepted by these people, a sense of "rightness" that would have alarmed him if he had stopped to think about it.

The second surprise came when the house lights went down; he actually found himself looking toward the stage with a sense of anticipation. The orchestra played first, a selection of short pieces picked, Grant decided, to allow the children a chance to shine without taxing their musical ability too much. He clapped as loudly as anyone when they took their bows, increasing the volume when Sean stood up with the horn section to be applauded. And then the curtains opened and the play itself began.

He held his breath when Lizzie made her entrance, concerned that everything should go right for her. She played her part with endearing gravity, delivering her one word—"Corn"—in a deadly serious voice as she set her basket on the Thanksgiving table. That done, she clasped her braids tightly, one in each hand, and backed away to stand with the group of other pint-size Indians who had already made their offerings to the Pilgrims. A funny little lump formed in Grant's throat. He coughed softly to clear it.

"Oh, Lord. I can't stand it," Lily whispered in a strangled voice.

He glanced sideways to see her wiping at her eyes with her fingertips.

"I'm sorry," she murmured self-consciously. "It's just that she's so little and this is her first play."

Grant bent his head. "Her day-butte," he whispered in her ear, imitating Lizzie's pronunciation of the word.

Lily gave a watery little giggle that ended in an almost sob. "Oh, please." She dabbed at her eyes again. "Don't get me started. My mascara's probably already all over my face."

He lifted her chin with his finger. "Looks fine to me." Their gaze locked for a charged moment, then broke apart. He dropped his hand from her chin and reached inside his jacket. "Here. Use this," he said, pressing a folded cotton handkerchief into her hand.

Stupid move, Saxon, he berated himself, staring straight ahead. His body was on fire. Just one look, one touch of her silky skin and he felt like a teenager in heat. *Dammit,* he told himself, refusing to give in and look at her again, *I knew this would happen if I came.*

Lily sat very still beside him, forcing herself to keep her eyes on the stage. *All he has to do is touch me and I fall apart,* she thought despairingly, wondering what it was about him that drew her so strongly.

He was almost sinfully good-looking, true, but she wasn't the type to have her head turned by a pretty face. He was intelligent, but she could name any number of men who were at least as smart. He was kind to the children. He was adventurous. He was reckless. And he would be gone as soon as he'd gathered enough material for his article.

And I want him, anyway. Her fist clenched around the handkerchief in her hand. *Desperately.*

The thought shocked her right down to her toes. It was so unlike her. She had never been the type of woman who counted the world well lost for love, never been one who threw her heart headlong into the fray with no thought for where it might lead her.

"Passionless," Jeffrey had called her when he was explaining why he wanted a divorce. And she'd agreed with him. At its best, making love with her husband had been pleasantly cozy and comfortable. At its worst it had been another chore. But it had never been something she thought about to the exclusion of all else, even in the beginning.

Why did Grant's slightest touch turn her blood to fire?

"Mom?" Jeff poked her in the arm. "Hey, Mom, you okay?"

Lily blinked and looked around, realizing that the Thanksgiving Pageant was almost over. The orchestra was playing the last chorus of "God Bless America," the children on the stage had joined hands to sing the words of the song, and the audience was getting to its feet, applauding their offspring enthusiastically. Lily jumped up and joined them, smiling reassuringly at her son as she dashed the remnants of tears from her eyes.

But were they tears of motherly sentiment, she wondered, or tears of frustrated desire?

"WOULD YOU LIKE to come in for hot chocolate and cookies?" Lily asked, glancing at Grant across the width of the front seat as she pulled up behind the lodge and set the parking brake. She told herself it was mere politeness that prompted her to issue the invitation. But the truth was that she couldn't bear to say good-night. Not yet.

Grant surprised himself with his reply. "Make that coffee and you're on," he said, completely disregarding the fact that he'd spent the half-hour ride back from the grade-school auditorium telling himself all the reasons that continued fraternizing would be hazardous to both of them.

He told himself—repeatedly—that Lily Talbot wasn't a woman who could, or would, indulge in a no-strings-attached affair. And he was a man who indulged in no other kind. They simply were not meant to be; however much his body burned for hers it was better—*kinder*—not to start anything. He knew all that, and yet . . .

And yet she's so damned sweet, he thought almost irritably, as if somehow her sweetness were a deliberate lure set out to trap him. *So warm and soft. And so damned giving.* If he reached out and took, would she give some of that warmth and softness to him?

No, he'd tried that already, he reminded himself. And she'd quite rightly pulled back before they'd gone too far.

So why was she inviting him in now? he wondered, absently reaching out to lift Elizabeth from the back seat of the car. Was she giving him some sort of signal, some nonverbal sign to encourage him to try his luck again? Was she hinting that this time she might not stop him?

Oh, hell, Saxon, he thought then, disgusted with himself. *Get your mind out of the gutter! She's invited you for exactly what she said—hot chocolate and cookies. Besides, you can't do any taking, and she sure as hell can't do any giving with three kids in the room.*

Elizabeth squirmed, babbling something unintelligible right next to his ear.

"I'm sorry, sweetheart." He refocused his gaze on the child he still held in his arms. "What did you say?"

"Put me down," she instructed imperiously, impatient with his dawdling.

Grant flushed. He'd been standing there thinking impure thoughts about their mother and blocking the door while the kids were trying to get out of the car. "Sorry," he mumbled, setting her on her feet beside the Blazer. He stepped back to allow Sean to get out.

Sean held out his hand to be helped down, too. "Mom made chocolate-chip cookies today," the little boy said, smiling up at Grant as he hopped to the ground.

"Yeah?" Grant answered, automatically holding out his hand to the last occupant of the back seat. Jeff glared at him for a full second, then deliberately turned his head and slid out the opposite door. He slammed it shut.

"Uh-huh," Sean chattered on, falling into step beside Grant as they ascended the back steps. "Chocolate chip are my favorite. What's yours?"

"I like chocolate chip, too," Grant answered absently, his eyes on the sulky teenager who raced up the steps ahead of them. The screen door banged against the doorframe with unnecessary force.

What the hell's the matter with him, Grant wondered.

"Jeff's mad about something," Sean confided then, as if he had read Grant's mind.

"Oh?" *Talk about understatement!* "About what?"

Sean shrugged; the peculiarities of his elder brother were beyond the scope of his ten-year-old mind. "Mom says it's his age." He sighed. "We're supposed to be understanding, she said, and not get mad back." Clearly Sean found such a task onerous. "We're just supposed to just ignore it," he told Grant.

"Okay," Grant agreed, hiding a grin at the boy's long-suffering expression. "Let's just ignore it, then."

They entered the kitchen. The large cheery room was already redolent with the mingled scents of brewing coffee and hot chocolate warming on the stove. Lily stood with her back to the door, reaching up into an open cupboard, her head slightly turned to keep an eye on Elizabeth as she stood on a chair arranging cookies on a plate. Lily's fuzzy shawl was folded over the back of a kitchen chair, leaving the gray sweater dress free to outline the slender curves of the body beneath it as she stood on tiptoe to reach a set of ceramic mugs. Jeff was nowhere to be seen.

"Here, let me get those for you," Grant said, moving quickly. He reached above her head, his arm duplicating the position of hers. The soft, upswept tendrils of her hair brushed against his chin. Her sweet wildflower scent curled in his nostrils. "These the ones you want?" he croaked hoarsely, trying to stifle his body's instant reaction to her nearness.

"Yes." Lily's voice was just as husky as his, but softer. She sidled away from the temptation of him, fighting the urge to lean back into the warmth of his big body. *When was the last time someone held me like that, in that snug way with his arms wrapped around me from behind?* she wondered wistfully, ducking her head to free herself from the sensual prison of his upraised arm. Her hips brushed against the front of his jeans.

"Those—" She cleared the sudden obstruction from her throat, color flooding her cheeks as she felt his body's response—and the instant, answering receptiveness of her own. "Those are the ones."

She whirled toward the stove to hide her blush. "Just set them on the counter there. The chocolate will be done in a minute. And the coffee. Sean, go tell your brother that if he wants some hot chocolate and cookies, he'd better get in here now." She risked a glance over her shoulder at Grant. "Go ahead and sit down," she invited, looking back at the chocolate she was furiously stirring. "You, too, Lizzie. It'll be ready in a minute."

Grant was only too glad to accept her invitation. *Good God, how was a man supposed to handle the physical realities of male sexual response surrounded by a houseful of kids?* he wondered, sliding into a chair. *What the hell did a family man do when he was suddenly turned on by his wife in front of the kids?* He glanced at Lizzie to see if she'd noticed anything amiss. *Wouldn't want to warp her delicate little psyche,* he thought.

But Elizabeth hadn't noticed anything amiss. She finished arranging the cookies to her satisfaction, jumped down from the chair and turned to carefully lift the laden plate off the counter. She set it on the table with a triumphant little smile and scrambled into her chair.

"Jeff says he'll be here in a minute," Sean announced, slipping into his place at the table. "He said he has to get his homework first."

"Homework?" Lily placed a mug of chocolate in front of each child. "I thought he didn't have any for tomorrow."

Sean shrugged and reached for his mug, dragging it across the table to blow across its surface.

"I thought you didn't have any homework," Lily said as Jeff came into the room with a textbook and notepad in the crook of his arm. She set his mug of chocolate on the table.

"Forgot about it," he mumbled, dropping into his chair. The textbook landed on the table with a thud, just short of actually being slammed down. He studiously avoided looking at Grant. It was obvious that the boy thought he had no business being there.

And you're right, kid, I don't, Grant thought, wondering how Lily was going to handle her son's deliberate rudeness. His own mother would have read him the riot act right there in front of everybody and, as far as he could tell, Lily was another one exactly like his mother, determined to raise her kids right, with proper manners and respect for their elders. He almost had it in him to feel sorry for the poor kid.

But Lily surprised him. She gave her son a sharp, penetrating look but issued no reprimand.

Now was not the time to bring up the subject of his unhappiness over Cynthia's new baby, she thought, sympathizing with his confusion over the subject. She'd talk to him about it later, when she went in to say goodnight to the boys. Sean would probably benefit from some discussion, too; all three of the kids would. They had to be wondering how their father's new baby was going to affect his relationship with them.

It never occurred to her that Jeff's bad mood had nothing to do with his soon-to-be born half brother or sister and everything to do with the brown-eyed man sitting at her kitchen table.

"Which class is the homework for?" she asked mildly, turning back to the counter to pour coffee for her and Grant.

"Geography."

"Mrs. Matlock's class?" She slid into the chair beside him.

"Uh-huh."

She folded her hands around the coffee cup. "What are you studying?"

"South America."

"What part of South America?"

"The Amazon Basin."

Lily looked across the table at Grant. "You've been there, haven't you, Grant?" she said. "I remember reading a big piece in, oh, I think it was *National Geographic*, a while back." She smiled at her son. "I'm sure Mr. Saxon could tell you about lots of things that the textbook doesn't even mention."

Jeff shot up out of his chair. "I'm gonna go study in my room," he said and stomped out of the kitchen.

A small, tense silence followed in his wake.

"I'm sorry about that," Lily said with a slight shake of her head. "He's not usually so rude and—" she shrugged "—something's bothering him."

Yeah, thought Grant, *and I'm that something.*

Well, don't worry, kid, he telegraphed silently, *I won't be around long enough to cause any real trouble. For either of us.*

7

THANKSGIVING DAY dawned drizzly and cold and lonesome. The children had left for their father's right after school the previous day. Tim was in California with his family. Even Art Fairfax and Bob Landers, the two fishermen from cabin one, had gone, and only one of Lily's cabins was occupied now: cabin four.

She tried to stay out of the kitchen, away from the temptation of the window, and for a while she was successful.

She spent the early part of the day doing all the little personal tasks that usually went undone because of the children or paying guests or both. She took a long, hot bubble bath first, lolling in the old-fashioned claw-footed tub until the bathroom mirrors were steamy. She conditioned her hair and shaved her legs and, finally, settled down in front of the massive old fireplace in her bedroom to give herself a long-neglected pedicure while she watched the Thanksgiving Day parade on TV. But all too soon the parade was over and her toenails were dry and her hair was curling softly on her shoulders, gleaming from the conditioner she had used. And she was bored and restless and lonely.

Now what? she thought restively, shutting off the television to wander through the empty rooms of the lodge. She tweaked the corner of a sofa pillow as she passed it, pinched off a discolored leaf on the English ivy that was crawling up the bookcase, peeked into the children's rooms to see if there were any housekeeping chores that needed to be done. But she had done them all last night, after Jeff and Sean and Lizzie had boarded the bus to Portland.

She sat down at her scarred old rolltop to work on the resort's books for a while, but she was as meticulous a bookkeeper as she was a housekeeper and it took her less than fifteen minutes to bring the ledger totally up-to-date.

She tried to settle down with a magazine, telling herself that this was a perfect time to catch up on her reading.

"Oh, hell," she said aloud, uttering a rare curse word. "Who needs another twenty recipes for Christmas cookies?" She tossed the magazine on the sturdy oak coffee table and stalked into the kitchen. "I will not let that man destroy my holiday," she muttered to herself, crouching to haul the roasting pan out of a lower cupboard. She always had a traditional Thanksgiving meal, children or no children, and she was going to have one today!

Methodically, eyes focused directly on her task, she prepared the turkey breast for the oven, gently spooning the chestnut stuffing under the carefully loosened skin. Sweet potatoes were peeled and quartered, then layered into a small casserole with crushed pecans, brown sugar, nutmeg and butter. Pint jars of home-canned vegetables sat on the kitchen counter, needing only heating at the last minute. Parker House rolls were put to rise near the warmth of the stove. A chocolate-cream pie, piled high with a glossy meringue, waited on a shelf in the refrigerator. Tangy orange-cranberry relish, covered with plastic wrap, waited beside it.

There, she thought with satisfaction when all her preparations were done and the smell of roasting turkey filled the kitchen. *I have enough food to feed—* Her thoughts faltered, the hand that had been wielding a dishcloth over the counter stopped in midmotion. "To feed a hungry man," she finished aloud, suddenly realizing exactly what she had been leading up to with all her careful preparations—both culinary and otherwise.

She was going to invite Grant Saxon to share her Thanksgiving dinner with her. And then she was going to invite him to share her bed.

The thought brought no start of surprise with it. Surprise would have meant that the idea was a new one. And it wasn't. She had first thought about it—tentatively, hesitantly, shocked at the very idea—in the long, wakeful night after the Thanksgiving Pageant.

The children would be at their father's, her wanting body whispered, the lodge would be empty, no one would ever have to know that Lily Talbot had broken her own rules of proper conduct and made love to a man for no reason other than that she wanted him. And even if someone did know, so what? She was a grown woman, with a grown woman's needs and desires. No one would think any less of her in this day and age if she took a lover, as long as she didn't do it in front of the children. Dawn, of course, had brought a return of common sense and a denial of the lonely nighttime desires, and she had put the idea firmly out of her mind.

But now it was back, staring her in the face in the cold light of day.

"And why shouldn't I?" she said defiantly, throwing the dishcloth into the corner of the sink. "I want him. Why shouldn't I?"

Especially as he was the only man she had ever wanted that way. Passionately. Desperately. So much so that she thought she might curl up and die if she didn't have him.

And all this...this *feeling*, she marveled, from a woman who had long ago decided she wasn't the passionate type. A woman whose husband had asked for a divorce because, he'd said, she treated him more like one of her children than the man she had conceived those children with. And it was true; she admitted it freely. She was more mother than wife, and had been content to have it so.

Only now she wasn't content at all, she thought despairingly, her eyes turning to the window. Because the last thing she wanted to do with Grant Saxon was mother him!

She picked the dishcloth up out of the sink and folded it carefully, hanging it in its place over the water faucet. She took off her apron, smoothing a hand down its length after she had hung it on its hook. Then, without even pausing to look in the mirror that hung over the coatrack by the back door, she stepped out into the freezing November day and walked purposefully across the yard to cabin four.

Grant saw her coming from his place by the window and hurried to open the door before she could raise her hand to knock. "What the hell are you doing here?" he growled irritably, flinging the door back to let her in. If she'd come over to indulge in another bout of kiss 'n' cuddle without going any further, he wouldn't be able to stand it. Nor would he be answerable for the consequences.

Lily halted in the doorway, all her newfound courage disappearing in the face of his scowl. "I'm sorry. I'll go."

"No!" He grabbed her arm and dragged her inside. "I didn't mean to snarl at you. I have this—" he ran a hand through his chestnut hair "—this damned article is giving me fits." *Because I can't concentrate on anything but you.* He dropped his hand from her arm as soon as she was safe inside. Touching her did strange, savage things to his gut. "Now what can I do for you?" he said in a more normal voice.

"Well, I, ah . . ." *Go ahead*, she told herself sternly. *Ask him.* "I've got a turkey that's about to come out of the oven and a chocolate-cream pie in the fridge and no one to help me eat it." She looked up at him, the invitation clear if he cared to see it. She moistened her lips nervously before continuing. "Would you be interested?"

"Chocolate-cream pie?" he said inanely, watching the quick, flickering movement of her tongue. Was she suggesting what he thought she was suggesting? Or was it just a simple offer to share Thanksgiving dinner and nothing more? Either way, it wouldn't be wise to take her up on it, not the way he was feeling. But, dammit, he thought, staring into her guileless blue eyes, either way, *whatever* she was offering, he wanted it. Badly.

If it was just a meal and conversation, okay, he could handle it; if it was a little necking on the living-room couch after dinner, well, he was desperate enough to take what he could get. And if she offered everything— No, better not think about everything or all his good intentions would end up tangled on the floor between them.

He'd let her set the pace, he told himself, let her lead the way to whatever was—or was not—going to happen between them. He wouldn't push or cajole or get down on his knees and beg. He hoped.

"Just let me get my shoes on." He turned abruptly, grabbing his hiking boots with one hand as he sat down on the edge of the bed to put them on.

"I have candied sweet potatoes, too," Lily said, needing to say something to fill the silence while he bent his head over the laces of his shoes. "And homemade cranberry relish and Parker House rolls and—"

"Stop," Grant ordered, springing to his feet. "You're making me drool all over myself." *In more ways than one*, he added mentally, striding across the room to the door. He opened it eagerly, ushering her out ahead of him. "Okay, lead me to this feast of yours." They stepped off the sheltered porch into a fine drizzling sleet. He grabbed her hand. "Run for it!" he hollered, dragging her along behind him.

They stumbled into Lily's warm, fragrant kitchen, laughing and out of breath and suddenly, inexplicably, the very best of companions. Somehow, now that the invitation had been made and accepted—however silently, however obliquely—some of the awful tension went out of both of them.

"It's freezing out there," Grant complained, rubbing his upper arms with his palms. "The temperature must have dropped ten degrees in the past hour or so. And I haven't got my long johns on."

"Sissy." She shook her head, laughing at him as she pulled the utility-room door closed to hold in the kitchen's heat. It amused her to think that a man who dismissed a broken leg as nothing would quail at a little cold weather. "You won't need your long johns in here," she assured him. "No matter how bad it gets out there." She glanced out the window as she passed it. "Maybe it'll turn to snow," she said hopefully, standing on tiptoe to get at her best china plates. "We could sure use it."

"Do you depend on the skiers for much of your business?" Grant asked, taking the plates from her to set them on the table. He hadn't thought much about her business before, only her. Now, remembering the rows of bread baked for sale, the home-canned vegetables, the five-year-old Blazer she drove, he wondered if things were hard for her financially.

"The skiers usually manage to keep the cabins full during the winter," she said, reaching up for the crystal wineglasses that had been among her wedding gifts. "Especially over the holidays if the snow is good. And it's usually very good," she added, glancing at him over her shoulder. He averted his eyes from her jeans-clad rear end. "This year's snowfall has been off," she continued, "but it really hasn't hurt me too much because winter's not my busiest season. Summer is." She got cutlery from one drawer, dark blue linen napkins from another. "The cabins are always full then and most of the campsites. There're thirty."

"Where?"

"They're scattered out in the woods behind the cabins." She closed the drawer with her hip. "There's a bottle of wine in the fridge," she said, scooping up the plates that Grant had set on the table. "Chenin Blanc. The opener's in that drawer next to the sink. We have time for one glass before dinner has to be seen to." She went into the living room and began arranging the china and cutlery on the coffee table in front of the fireplace. Grant followed her a moment later.

"Is this stuff any good?" asked Grant suspiciously, sniffing the top of the bottle with a Californian's innate distrust of any non-California wine.

"Don't be a snob," Lily chided, smiling as she took the bottle from him. "Oregon vineyards grow some excellent wines." Firelight danced on the glasses as she filled them, turning their contents to pale gold. "Especially whites. I've been told it has something to do with the weather being like Germany's." She picked up both glasses, handing him one as she sat down on the overstuffed sofa. "Sit down," she invited as she lifted the glass to her lips. "Make yourself comfortable."

Grant sat down next to her, close enough to smell her perfume but not so close that he couldn't see her sweet, smiling face.

"So," she said then, settling back into the corner of the sofa with the glass cradled in her palm. "Tell me about yourself."

"What would you like to know?"

"Oh, I don't know," she lied. She wanted to know everything—every thought, every feeling, every tiny bit of his life history. "How old are you?"

He leaned back, smiling at the ingenuous way she asked the question. "Thirty-six. How old are you?"

"Thirty-two."

His lips pursed, and he shook his head in mock disapproval. "And Jeff's what? Thirteen? Fourteen? You must have cut it pretty close."

"He's thirteen. And you have a dirty mind," she chided, laughing. "I'll have you know he's entirely legitimate. I was married two days after my high school graduation, and Jeff was born exactly nine months to the day later."

Grant crossed his right ankle over his opposite knee, and took another sip of his wine. "Then why the hurry to get married if you didn't have to? Didn't you want to go to college? Experience some of the world before settling down?"

Lily shook her head. "All I ever wanted was to be married and have children," she said, running a fingertip around the rim of her glass. She knew a man like Grant might laugh at her life's ambition, but it was the truth. "There didn't seem to be any reason to do anything else first."

"No regrets for all you missed?"

"You're assuming that I feel I've missed something." Her tone held just a touch of asperity. "I haven't. I've done exactly what I've wanted to do with my life." She looked at him over her wineglass. "Have you?"

The question caught him unawares. Had he? Really? Did he honestly enjoy living out of a suitcase or a backpack? Did he actually like breaking some bone or other every year or so? Did he get a kick out of portaging a canoe around a too-swift rapids in some South American river while inhaling air that was almost too liquid to breathe? Or freezing his buns off competing in some obscure cross-country ski race? He had once—there was no doubt about that. But lately? It wasn't something he wanted to think about.

"I do what I want to do, when I want to do it," he said a touch defiantly. "And when I don't want to do it anymore," he added, "I'll quit."

So there! Lily added mentally. "And do what?" she said.

"Do what when?"

"When you quit doing what you're doing now."

He shrugged against the sofa, the subtle movement stretching the soft fabric of his flannel shirt tight across his chest and shoulders. "Maybe I'll take a crack at that book Neil keeps nagging me to write. But that's still a long way off."

"A book? How exciting. What will it be—"

A buzzer went off in the kitchen.

"That'll be the turkey," she said, getting to her feet. She set her wineglass on the table. "No, you stay right there." She put a hand on his shoulder, pushing him back against the sofa. "Have another glass of wine and enjoy the fire. It'll take me ten minutes or so to get dinner together, so make yourself at home," she advised, disappearing into the kitchen.

She returned to the living room fifteen minutes later to find that Grant had taken her advice. The heavy woven drapes had been drawn back from the long windows on either side of the fireplace. The old pewter candlesticks that usually stood on either end of the mantel now sat in the middle of the coffee table, their fat cream-colored candles adding their own special glow to the setting. His shoes stood, side by side, at one end of the sofa.

"I hope you don't mind," he said, turning from the window as she came into the room. Sleet, mixed now and then with a fat, wet snowflake, beat against the glass behind him, making the room seem all the more cozy and warm.

"No, I don't mind at all. It looks lovely."

"Let me take that for you." He reached out for the laden tray that she carried. "On the table here?"

"Yes, that'll be fine. Thank you.

They settled down on the floor on opposite sides of the coffee table and smiled at each other over the glow of the candlelight. Without a word Lily rose to her knees and began filling their plates.

Perfect slices of turkey breast, cut so that the chestnut filling made a strip at the top, nestled on the white china plates next to sweet potatoes made glossy with a sugary glaze and crunchy with nuts. Home-canned corn, green beans and cranberry relish each added their own touch of color. Warm yeast rolls were offered from a napkin-lined basket, butter from a chilled crock.

Grant looked down at the laden plate placed in front of him. "At the risk of repeating myself, may I say that this looks absolutely delicious?"

"You may." Lily smiled as she settled back down on her hip. Then she picked up her wineglass and lifted it toward him in a toast. "Happy Thanksgiving, Grant," she said softly.

He touched his glass to hers over the table. "Happy Thanksgiving, Lily," he echoed just as softly.

Their eyes held as they drank.

"Tell me what your book will be about," Lily invited then, putting down her wineglass to pick up her fork.

"*If* I write it, it'll probably be set in the Amazon and involve unscrupulous land developers, a few government nasties and an intrepid hero who's trying to save the rain forest from high-rise condos and shopping malls, with maybe a little local revolution thrown in so it doesn't get boring." He shrugged disparagingly. "All the usual adventure-suspense stuff."

"If you write it?"

"I haven't actually decided to do it."

"But why not? It sounds wonderful."

"I'm not ready to retire yet," Grant told her, launching into an account of all the things he wanted to do before he settled down to something as sedentary as writing a novel. Subtly he was reminding her—and himself—that he was a free man, not one to be tied down to any one place, or any one woman. Lily understood.

So she kept the conversation light, chuckling and ahhing at his anecdotes, telling some of her own, carrying them easily, companionably, through dinner and dessert and the mutual cleanup of the kitchen all the way to the brandy that Grant was warming between his palms.

And now it's time, she thought, accepting the snifter he offered her. She could see it in his eyes; he wanted to make love to her; he *would* make love to her if she'd let him, now that he knew she understood that that's all it would be. He was only waiting for a sign from her. And she wanted to give it to him. Oh, how she wanted to. But not yet. Not . . . here.

The lodge was full of memories of the children. Of her role as a mother and homemaker. There on the sofa was where she heard about Jeff's day at school or Sean's latest triumph on the soccer field. It was where she sat and darned socks and watched the kids play Monopoly or Old Maid or Go Fish. They roasted marshmallows in the fireplace together sometimes and popped corn with the old-fashioned popper that she'd found at a country flea market. And the bed in her room, with the fireplace blazing cozily in front of it . . . well, Lizzie was still young enough to want to come and snuggle with her mother on Sunday mornings.

Could the memories of Grant Saxon's illicit lovemaking coexist in the same bed with the whispered confidences of her daughter?

No.

So maybe it wouldn't happen after all. Maybe it shouldn't. She sighed, her eyes wandering past Grant to one of the long windows that flanked the fireplace. The sleet had turned to snow. Big, fat, fluffy flakes of snow, falling steadily out of a lowering sky. It was the sticking kind; the trees were already wearing a veil of white, and the ground looked as if it had been dusted with powdered sugar. Inspiration struck.

"Grant." She touched the back of his hand lightly, hesitantly, calling his attention from the flames dancing in the fireplace.

He turned his head against the sofa, his eyes lifting to hers. Smoldering, questioning, rife with unspoken longing.

"Let's go camping."

"Camping?"

"Yes, camping," she said, suddenly sure that that was the answer. "It's snowing. The woods will be beautiful. And we wouldn't have to go far. Only to one of the campsites out back. I have all the equipment: A pup tent. Sleeping bags. It'll be fun," she rambled on when he didn't answer. "Besides, you're supposed to be writing an article on the beauties of Oregon's forests, aren't you?" She gave him a tremulous little smile. "You ought to get a firsthand look at them."

He ignored all her reasons except the unspoken one. "Do you know what will happen if we do?"

"Yes, I know."

"We'll only use one sleeping bag, Lily."

"I know."

"I won't be offering you anything permanent. No commitment," he warned her. "No happily-ever-after."

"I know."

"And you still want to risk it?"

"Yes."

Grant picked up her free hand from the sofa between them and raised it to his lips. "Then let's go camping."

8

THAT NIGHT, in the cozy shelter of a one-man pup tent, with a double sleeping bag warming the ground beneath them and a gentle snow blanketing the world in silence, Grant and Lily became lovers. It was far easier than she had ever imagined it would be, far easier than it had been the first time she'd disrobed for a man. There was no shyness, no embarrassing hesitation, no painful awkwardness to mar the moment. There was only joy and tenderness and a depth of passion that astounded her.

Grant undressed himself first—quickly and matter-of-factly—and then he began to undress her. Slowly, gently, as they lay side by side, he praised and touched and kissed each bit of skin as it was revealed to him.

"You have beautiful shoulders, Lily. Like polished ivory," he murmured, brushing his open mouth across them. "And such soft, soft skin." Four fingertips trailed down the side of her body to her waist and back up again, raising a shiver in their wake. "And your breasts..." He kissed each rosy nipple as he peeled back the cups of her bra. "Ah, Lily, I could write poetry to your breasts," he sighed, nuzzling his face between them. "So soft. So sweet. So womanly." His intoxicating words were punctuated by tiny, openmouthed kisses, each one placed farther down her torso than the last, until his chin was nudging against the waistband of her jeans. "So smooth all over." He pulled the snap open with his teeth.

"I . . . I have stretch marks," she warned breathlessly, catching her bottom lip in her teeth as he slowly lowered the zipper. Her blood was buzzing in her ears, her bones slowly dissolving as he explored her.

"What? These tiny little lines?" He found the faint lines with his fingertips and traced them across her abdomen, fascinated by what they represented. None of his previous lovers had ever borne children, and he had never given any thought to what doing so would do to a woman's body, except, perhaps, to feel an undefined distaste for all it entailed. But these pale lines on Lily's stomach suddenly seemed to him to be the very essence of womanliness and warmth. "Love lines," he said solemnly, replacing his fingers with the tip of his tongue.

Lily felt her heart turn over with an emotion so intense that it was almost painful. "Grant," she murmured, reaching for him. Her hands touched his lean cheeks, feeling them move as he kissed her stomach. She stroked his hair, delighting in the way the chestnut strands curled around her fingers. She caressed the curve of his ears and the taut cords of his neck with careful, inquisitive hands. And then slowly, achingly slowly, to give herself the most pleasure possible, she smoothed her open palms over his wide shoulders and down his apple-hard biceps, up over his hair-dusted forearms to the hard, brown hands that lightly cupped the sides of her breasts. She pressed his hands inward and up, so that they covered her completely. His fingers flexed, kneading her flesh; his mouth opened over her navel. "Grant," she said again.

He lifted his head and looked up at her.

"Not enough," she said, answering the unasked question she saw there. The time for gentle foreplay was past. She was ready. Eager. As she had never been eager for the act of love before. "More."

Eyes blazing, he moved his body up over hers and took her mouth. His tongue thrust between her open lips. His thumbs rotated against her swollen nipples. She could feel his hardness pressing against her jeans-clad thigh. "Tell me you want me, Lily," he breathed against her mouth. He had to hear her say it. He had to be absolutely sure.

"I want you," she whispered.

"Again." One hand moved to her stomach, burrowing under the open front of her jeans and the pale blue panties beneath them. "Tell me again."

As naturally as breathing, she sucked in her stomach to give him easier access. "I want you," she said again, louder, gasping as his fingers found her. Her hips lifted. "So much."

"Then show me," he demanded. Pleaded. "Show me how much you want me."

She pushed against him then, reaching with both hands to shove her jeans and panties off her hips, sitting up to peel them off her legs and toss them into a corner of the small tent. Her shirt and bra followed. Then she lay back down on the sleeping bag and opened her legs to him. "I want you, Grant," she said clearly, her soft blue eyes holding his. Her arms lifted to gather him close. "Now."

"Oh, God, *Lily*." Quickly he fumbled through the pockets of his discarded jeans for the necessary protection, then lowered himself slowly, almost reverently, struggling to enter her gently, fighting the urge to thrust as fast and hard and deep as he wanted to. But she felt so good—so damned good!—that it was all he could do to keep it from being over the moment he slipped into her.

She could feel him trembling against her, feel the effort he was making to go slowly. For her sake. And it was so unnecessary; he had already given her more physical pleasure than she had ever had. "I won't break," she whispered, smoothing her hands down the long, hard muscles of his back.

"I want it to be good for you." The words hissed out through gritted teeth.

"It is good."

"I want it to be perfect."

"It is." Her hands scooped out the hollow at the small of his back, then slid over the curve of his buttocks. "It is."

His hands flexed on her shoulders. "Oh, God, Lily. I—" A strangled sound escaped him, and he stilled against her, fighting for control.

"It's okay," she soothed, lifting her hips, urging him to move as she knew he wanted to.

But still he delayed, going slowly until he had gained control of his raging body, then moving strongly, deeply, whispering thrilling, naughty love words in her ear until her sweat-sheened body was bowed as tightly as his and her breath was rasping in his ear.

"Oh, Grant . . . Grant." Her hands curled, her short nails leaving half-moon impressions on the hard curve of his buttocks. "*Please.*"

He let his body have its way then, plunging wildly into her willing, yearning moistness until they both cried their passion aloud.

Passion. It overwhelmed her. Engulfed her. Glorified her. It burst inside her body like a thousand Roman candles. Shattered her heart into a sparkling catherine wheel of pure emotion. She found herself sobbing in his arms when it was over.

"I d-didn't know," she gasped, still reeling from the aftershocks that rippled through her body. "It never happened to me before. Not l-like that, and . . . and . . . *Oh, Grant,*" she wailed, clutching him.

"Shh, Lily. It's all right." He rolled to his side, his big hand cradling the back of her head, and held her close. "It's all right," he soothed, his voice shaky with his own rolling emotions. He'd never had a woman react this way before, never had a woman burst into tears with the intensity of her release, and his heart was near to bursting with a strange mixture of masculine pride and a fierce, possessive tenderness.

Her first time, he thought as he lay there with her trembling in his arms. Twelve years of marriage and three kids and that was her first time. Just what in the hell kind of selfish jackass had she been married to? Grant was torn between wanting to murder the bastard—and wanting to thank him for leaving her so innocent. For leaving to Grant the intense pleasure of being the first man to lead her to full sexual climax. *Which probably makes me as selfish as he is*, Grant thought, hugging her tighter in silent apology.

Lily stirred restively then, putting up a hand to wipe her tears, and sniffled into his neck.

He loosened his hold on her. "All better now?" he said, coming up on his elbow to tenderly brush the damp hair away from her cheek.

She nodded but didn't look up. "Yes. Yes, I'm fine. I'm sorry I fell apart like that."

A strangled sound rumbled in his chest, half laugh, half groan. "Lily, you don't have to *apologize* for a response like that. Don't you know how it made me feel?" He drew back a little so he could look at her. "Do you have any idea what it did to me to have you turn into a wild woman in my arms?"

She felt herself blushing. *Wild woman.* "No."

"No, don't turn away. Look at me." He cupped her cheek in his palm, turning her face back up to his. His sparkling eyes were serious. "You made me feel ten feet tall, Lily. Ten goddamned feet tall."

"Really?"

"Yes." He dropped a soft kiss on her lips. "Really."

She smiled shyly. "You made me feel pretty good, too."

He grinned, "Yeah, I noticed." He reached down behind him and rubbed at a spot on his buttock. "I can still feel how good I made you feel. I'm probably going to need a tetanus shot."

"What!"

"A tetanus shot." His eyes were sparkling again, teasing her. "I've got five nail-shaped puncture wounds in each cheek of my ass."

Heat flamed in her face but her smile didn't falter. "Oh, you do not."

"Yes, I do." He flopped over on his stomach. "Take a look if you don't believe me."

Lily hesitated, then sat up, her head brushing against the sloping side of the tent as she moved to lean over his prone body. He was beautifully made, she thought, powerful even in repose. His shoulders were wide, rounded with muscles that flowed naturally into the smooth curve of his back. Her eyes traced the shallow indentation of his spine, down to the curving hollow that flared into the firm, slightly squared halves of his buttocks, to the long, lean legs lightly dusted with hair, the left one less hairy below the knee where his cast had rubbed.

"Do you see them?" he demanded.

She brought her eyes back to the area of his supposed wounds. "No."

He reached a hand around behind him. "They're right there." He stabbed at his hip with the tip of his index finger.

"What? These tiny little marks?" Five faint indentations—already fading—marred each buttock. "You're not even going to need a Band-Aid," she scoffed, feeling light-headed and giddy, in the grip of some emotion that she didn't dare put a name to. "Let alone a tetanus shot."

"The woman has no sympathy."

"Oh, that's what you want. Sympathy. Why didn't you say so?" She leaned over suddenly and placed a quick, soft kiss on the marks nearest her. "There. All better."

Grant squirmed against the sleeping bag. "Something else hurts now," he said, deadpan.

"Oh?" He could hear the laughter in her voice. "Is it going to need a tetanus shot?"

He flipped over and grabbed her arm, yanking her down beside him. "I'll tell you what it's going to need," he growled. Putting his lips to her ear, he whispered the exact prescription required for his particular ailment.

"Oh . . . oh, my," Lily said breathlessly, not knowing whether to be shocked or excited by his explicit words. Excitement won out. "Are you sure you want to risk it?" Her blue eyes were shining with a recklessness almost as bold as his. "I might scratch you again."

His body moved over hers, into hers. She arched reflexively, eager hands reaching to pull him close. Closer.

"You can scratch the flesh off my bones if you want to," he said.

"RISE AND SHINE, sleepyhead."

Grant mumbled something extremely rude and snuggled deeper into the double sleeping bag, trying to pull it over his head.

"Come on, drag your bones out of there. It's a beautiful morning. All snowy and white."

Grant opened one eye a slit. "Lily?"

"Um-hmm. Right here."

He lifted his head a fraction of an inch and squinted in the general direction of her voice. All he could see was the lump his feet made in the down sleeping bag. He lifted his head a little higher. Opened his eyes a tiny bit wider. Lily's kneeling form was silhouetted just inside the triangular opening of the tent. A gentle snow floated to earth behind her.

"'Zat coffee I smell?"

"Yes."

One hand appeared outside the sleeping bag. "Gimme."

She held the mug just out of his reach. "Are you awake enough not to spill it?"

"Yes," he lied.

He heard her laugh softly. "No, you're not. Come on—sit up and I'll give it to you."

His hand disappeared back under the cover for a moment, then, grumbling about the cold, he pushed himself to a semiupright position. "Gimme," he said again.

Lily put the mug into his hand. "Are you always so rude in the morning?"

"Yes." He wrapped his hand around the mug and took a deep, greedy swallow. Then another. He sat up a little straighter, shooting her a disgruntled look from under lowered brows. "Are you always so cheerful?"

"'Fraid so."

They smiled at each other then—happy, conspiratorial, sappy smiles—as if what each had just found out about the other pleased them in some special, secret way.

"Little Mary Sunshine," Grant said caressingly, reaching out to hook his free hand around the back of her neck.

"Grumpy," Lily countered, leaning forward to meet his lips.

"MY FATHER always wanted to travel," Grant said over his shoulder as they picked their way along the trail to the small lake that bordered the campgrounds on Lily's property. "But he never did because of my mother. At least, not the kind of traveling he wanted to do."

"What kind of traveling was that?" Lily inquired, head down as she tried to step exactly where he had. She had to stretch to match the length of his stride.

"Something other than the yearly trip to visit her family in Nebraska, that's for sure. He had a yen to see the 'wild places,' as he called them. It was his dream to experience Isak Dinesen's Africa but—" Grant's shoulders lifted in a shrug beneath his down jacket "—he never got farther than a dude ranch in Montana the summer I was fourteen. Careful, right here," he said, holding a snow-laden branch out of her way.

"So you went to Africa for him." She ducked under the branch, flashing a smile of thanks as she came up even with him. "And all the other wild places he never got to see."

Grant paused to consider that, his hand still holding the pine bough back. He had never thought of it quite that way. Never consciously made the connection between his father's thwarted dreams and his own way of life. But hearing Lily say it just now made sense. "Yeah, I guess so. In a way. But I wanted to see them for myself, too." He let the branch go and continued down the path to the lake.

"Why didn't your mother like to travel?" Lily asked then, falling in behind him, completely forgetting the schoolgirl game of trying to step in his footprints.

He shrugged again. "She was—I don't know exactly—timid, I guess, would be the best description. She was a wonderful woman in most ways. A good mother and all that, but she liked things to stay on an even keel. That was one of her favorite expressions: 'even keel.'" He snorted disparagingly. "Anything in her life that deviated from the norm made her nervous."

I'll bet she chewed her nails to the quick over you, then, Lily thought, but she didn't say anything.

"She was always saying 'There's no place like home.' You know—" he glanced back at her "—like Dorothy in *The Wizard of Oz*? It expressed her whole philosophy of life."

"And what expresses yours?"

Grant didn't even have to think about it. "He who travels fastest travels alone," he answered over his shoulder. "That's my philosophy of life in a nutshell," he added, wondering why it suddenly sounded so hollow. "What's yours?"

"Oh . . . 'Home is where the heart is' about sums it up for me, I guess," she said, hoping the quick shaft of pain she'd felt at his careless words wasn't obvious in her voice.

"No FAIR! No fair!" Lily ran shrieking from Grant's flank attack, throwing handfuls of snow behind her as she ran. "You stole my snowballs!"

"And you cheated by stockpiling," Grant retaliated, pelting her retreating back with her own illegal store of ammunition. "Cheaters never prosper," he reminded her, scoring a direct hit on the seat of her jeans.

Lily yelped and ducked into a small stand of trees and underbrush, zigging and zagging until she was sure he'd lost sight of her. Then she dropped to her knees, scrambling madly to assemble another cache of snowballs before he found her.

"Come out of there, you coward!" Grant hollered. Snowballs crashed against the trees at about the height her back would have been if she were standing. "I've got you surrounded."

Lily stifled a whoop of excited, nervous laughter and went on forming snowballs as fast as she could.

"It vill go badly for you vhen you are found," he warned. She could hear him stomping around through the brush, getting nearer. "Ha! I haf found your trail. You vill not escape me now."

Lily bolted to her feet. "Aii-eee!" she screamed, mooshing a soft snowball directly into his face before she turned and ran. There was a surprised exclamation from the man behind her, a muffled curse as she evaded capture, then the rapid pounding of feet as he gave chase.

She felt his fingers catch at the back of her jacket. Panting, shrieking with laughter, she changed direction and twisted out of his reach. There was a loud crash behind her, a grunt as he made contact with the snowy ground. Triumphant, she whirled around to taunt him. "Ha, ha, I win! I— Grant?"

He lay in a crumpled heap in the snow, clutching his leg below the knee.

"Grant? Grant! Oh, my God, your leg!" She scrambled back to him over the slippery, snow-covered ground, guilty panic replacing the childish glee of a moment before. She should have remembered his bad leg!

"Gotcha!"

She came crashing down on top of him as he snagged her ankle. He rolled over, pressing her into the snow beneath him.

"Why, you! You're not hurt at all!" She wriggled furiously, trying to get away. "You *tricked* me!"

"Guerrilla tactics," he said smugly, grinning down at her.

"And you call me a cheater!" She grappled for a handful of snow. "You're worse than a cheater. You're a sneaky, low-down—"

"Ah, ah, ah," he chided, pinning her wrists to the ground above her head with one hand. "It's not smart to call the guy who's holding you down nasty names." He picked up his own handful of snow and held it over her face. "Would you like to take that back?" he said pleasantly.

"Never!" Lily panted, her chest bellowing in and out with breathlessness and laughter.

He hefted the snowball as if weighing it. "It's very cold. Freezing, in fact. You won't like it."

"Do your worst," she said theatrically, tossing her head like a silent-movie heroine.

Grant's laugh rumbled against her. "Oh, I intend to. Let me see; should I rub this in your face the way you did to me? Or maybe—" he paused consideringly "—down the front of your blouse?" he said, his eyes dropping to her heaving chest.

Deliberately Lily arched against him. "You wouldn't really," she said, widening her eyes at him, "would you?"

"That's not going to save you."

She let her thighs fall open beneath his. "No?" she whispered, feeling him harden against her.

"No," he said, but he didn't sound too sure.

She rotated her hips against his.

He dropped the snowball. "Dammit, Lily," he groaned, reaching to cup her breast through her jacket. "You're cheating again."

She shook her head against the snow. "Guerrilla tactics," she murmured, just before his mouth took hers.

"IT WOULDN'T BE WORTH IT to spend all this time for just one article," Grant said, trying to explain his profession to her, "unless I was doing it on assignment for *Life* or *National Geographic* or one of the other biggies." He dropped an armload of deadwood by the campfire she was tending. "I plan to turn this trip into five or six pieces at least."

"But how can you do that? I mean, I thought when you wrote something for a magazine it had to be original."

"They will be." He grinned at her. "More or less."

"But . . ."

"The one I write for a ski magazine will highlight Mount Bachelor and all the cross-country trails. The *Backpacker* will get an article on roughing it in the Three Sisters Wilderness Area. Or I might try to sell a piece on winter steelhead fishing for a magazine like *Field and Stream*. It's called slant."

Lily nodded sagely. "That explains it."

"Explains what?"

"The way your mind works."

He tilted his head at her. "Huh?"

"Slanted," she said, grinning at him like a kid who has just told a successful knock-knock joke.

"HAVE YOU EVER been married, Grant?" Lily asked the question as they sat together in front of the campfire, sipping their final cups of coffee before crawling into the tent. They'd already thoroughly discussed their respective childhoods and the angst of their teen years. They knew each other's favorite color and middle name and most embarrassing moment. They'd even tiptoed delicately around the edges of discussing Lily's twelve-year marriage. Asking if he'd ever been married seemed like the next logical question. Besides, she wanted— had—to know.

"No."

"Have you ever lived with anyone?"

"No."

"Ever wanted to?"

He considered that one for a moment. Had he ever wanted to? Ever even thought he wanted to, until now? "No," he said, denying the last part of his thought.

She tilted her head against his shoulder to look up at him. "Why not?"

He slanted her a wary glance out of the corner of his eye. "What do you mean, 'Why not?'"

"Exactly that. Why not? Most people want someone special to share their life with. Someone to come home to at the end of the day." She shrugged with assumed casualness, trying to pretend that his answer wasn't really important. "He who travels fastest travels alone," he'd said. "No commitments, no strings," he'd said. But she wasn't trying to tie him down with her question. She was just . . . curious. Just curious, she repeated silently, knowing she was deceiving herself. "You know what I mean."

"I don't usually come home at the end of the day," he reminded her, staring into his cup of coffee. "Sometimes I don't come home for weeks or months at a time. And when I do I don't stay very long."

"Well, yes, *now* you don't," she persisted. "But someday you will. Don't you want to get married eventually?" Everyone wanted to get married eventually, didn't they? Even confirmed bachelors must long for hearth and home eventually.

He tossed his remaining coffee on the ground. "No," he said.

"ARE YOU SURE you've been camping before?" Lily gave him a sidelong glance as she wrapped potatoes in foil for baking.

"More times than I can count," he assured her blandly, leaning back against a tree stump as he watched her fix their dinner.

"Then how come you don't know the first thing about cooking over a campfire?"

"Because I don't know the first thing about cooking, period."

"So what do you eat when you're out in the wilds of Colorado or the African jungle or wherever? Nuts and berries?"

"Depends." He selected a carrot stick from the relish tray she had fixed and bit into it.

"On what?" She laid the potatoes in the glowing coals on the edge of the campfire and turned her attention to making a marinade for the two T-bone steaks that waited in the ice chest.

"On what kind of camping I'm doing. Last time I was in Africa we had waiters who took care of the food."

"Waiters! On a camping trip?"

"It was a high-class safari. Not real camping. And neither—" he waved his carrot stick in the air, indicating their campsite "—is this."

"It isn't?" she said, laughing at his superior expression.

He drew his brows together with mock disapproval. "Hell, no. Real camping is when you hike for miles and miles into the wilderness, carrying all your worldly goods in a backpack. In a backpack there's no room for steaks and aluminum foil and bottles of Cabernet Sauvignon," he informed her. "There's only room for essentials."

"Food isn't essential?"

"Sure, but it comes in little foil packets that weigh almost nothing. Just add water and eat. Very nutritious."

"Yuck," Lily said, getting up to fetch the steaks from the cooler. "Sounds awful."

"It is," he agreed, "but you don't have to cook it." His eyes followed her as she moved, zeroing in on the seat of her jeans as she bent over. *Damn, she has a sexy rear end.* "How long before dinner's ready?"

"Oh, the potatoes will be done in an hour or so." She snapped the plastic lid on the container holding the marinating steaks. "Hungry?"

"Starving." He stood suddenly and scooped her up in his arms. "I think I'll have dessert first."

"Jeff, NOW—he's my serious one. When he was a baby I used to call him the judge. You know, as in as sober as?" She sighed against Grant's bare shoulder. "He took the divorce harder than either of the other two."

Grant's hand smoothed up and down the gentle slope of her back. "In what way?" It felt good to be lying there with her like this, he thought idly, sharing their thoughts and emotions after making love. He'd never done it with any other woman. Never wanted to do it with any other woman because, he realized, he had never really cared what their deepest thoughts and feelings were.

"He had terrible nightmares for about six months after his father and I separated," Lily said softly, remembering. "He angered easily. His grades took a nosedive. And he became a discipline problem at school, mostly stealing little things from the other kids' desks during recess. All perfectly normal reactions to the situation, according to the family therapist, but that wasn't much comfort. It was awful to see him suffer like that, especially when it was something his father and I had done to him."

Grant's arm tightened around her. "Is he all right now?" Are *you* all right now is what he really meant.

"Oh, yes, he's fine. Aside from a tendency to take life a little too seriously, that is. He thinks of himself as the man of the family. It's only natural, of course, because of the divorce and being the eldest and all. He's very protective of Sean and Lizzie. And of me, too, for that matter. In fact—" she laughed softly and pushed herself up on her elbow to look down at him "—we had a little talk before he left for his dad's. I thought he was upset because of Cynthia's pregnancy. That he might be worried that a new baby would take all his father's attention, but that wasn't it at all."

"No?"

"Uh-uh." She touched her fingertip to his nose. "It was you."

Surprise pulled his eyebrows together. "Me?"

Lily chuckled. "My elder son doesn't like the way you look at me."

"What!"

"'I don't like the way that Mr. Saxon looks at you, Mom' were his exact words. He thought maybe I should go with them to Portland in case you got any ideas about me being here all alone."

"Perceptive kid," Grant said, grinning up at her.

"Course, I didn't tell him that I had ideas about you, too," she admitted coyly.

"Yeah?" Sensual interest flared in his eyes. "What kind of ideas?"

"Oh..." Her fingers tiptoed down his flat belly. "Just ideas."

"Tell me."

She shrugged self-consciously and looked away, her fingers plucking delicately at the hairs around his navel.

"Shall I tell you some of mine first?"

She flashed him a quick glance from under her lashes, unable to hide the flicker of guilty excitement his suggestion generated in her. Jeffrey had never been one to talk about...things. She shrugged again, as if she didn't really care—but she didn't say no.

"That first night," he said, his voice husky with growing arousal, "there in your kitchen, I had fantasies about what you were wearing under your robe."

"My nightgown!" she interjected, blushing.

"I imagined what your breasts would look like," he said, ignoring her interruption. "What color your nipples would be." His hand stroked slowly, sensuously up and down her back while he talked. "How they would feel if I ran my tongue over them. How they would taste."

Lily sucked in her breath, feeling her nipples pucker and harden as if he had touched them.

"While you were drying my hair, I pictured you standing there completely naked."

Lily's breathing deepened erratically. Her fingers flexed against his stomach.

"It was all I could do to keep from leaning forward and taking a bite out of you. I dreamed about you that night."

Heat pooled between her thighs.

"I was dreaming about you when you knocked on my door the next morning." He fell silent, waiting.

"When you answered the door wearing nothing but that bedspread," she began timidly, "I thought . . ."

"Go on," he encouraged, his eyes avid. His hand was motionless on her back. "You thought what?"

She wet her lips with the tip of her tongue. "I thought you had the most magnificent chest I'd ever seen—all hard and tanned and hairy." She ran her palm over him adoringly as she spoke, not even realizing she was doing it. "And I wanted to reach out and yank the bedspread off to see if everything else was as beautiful."

"And?"

She lifted her eyes to his. "And it is. You are," she breathed. "Absolutely magnificent."

"So are you." His hand tightened on her back, his arms enfolded her, lifting her over him so that her breasts were crushed against his chest. "You're so soft and sweet and loving." He lifted his head and buried his lips in her throat. "So giving." His hands slid down her spine to her hips, pulling her tight against him. Her knees parted, sliding down to settle on either side of his body. "So *hot*," he groaned, feeling her moistness and heat pressed against him. He thrust upward, entering her.

"For you," she whispered into his hair, cradling his head as he mouthed her breast. "Only for you."

His hands urged her upright, tightening on her hips to show her the movement he craved.

He's a loner, she reminded herself, taking the movement for her own, rotating her pelvis to give him even more pleasure. His hands slid to her breasts then, palms cupping them, thumbs loving the crests to aching hardness. Her back arched, her head falling back as passion poured through her.

No strings, she chanted silently, moaning aloud as the feeling inside her struggled to break free. His hand moved between their straining bodies, seeking and finding the hidden nub of her femininity. She stiffened and tensed, ripples of sensation chasing along her skin as her climax took her past all reason, all thought.

"I love you," she whispered softly, achingly, helplessly, not even realizing that she'd spoken aloud. "Oh, Grant, darling, I love you."

9

GRANT WAS THE FIRST to realize what she had said. When her slender body had softened and relaxed, seeming to float down to rest against his chest, and his own breathing had returned to normal, the words she had whispered echoed through his mind with startling clarity.

"Oh, Grant, darling, I love you."

His first reaction was joy. A joy so intense that it threatened to choke him. *I love you, too, Lily,* he thought. And then panic set in; the awful sensation of being trapped in a net of his own making.

What in hell are you thinking about, Saxon?

It wasn't love he was feeling, he told himself sternly. Hell, no. It was lust, pure and simple. Lily Talbot was the sexiest woman he had ever made love to, that's all. And he was feeling... Feeling what? Grateful—that was it. Grateful for a sublime sexual experience. Appreciative of the fact that she had shared herself with him, in a way that she had with no one else. What man wouldn't be grateful? And full of loving feelings? But not in love. Never in love. Because being in love with Lily would mean changing his whole life. It would mean lifelong commitment, responsibilities, ties to one place.

It would mean kids, dammit all to hell! Three kids! *But I'm not in love with her*, he told himself. *I'm not.*

Lily felt his body change beneath her, subtly, in a way she couldn't quite understand with her mind but that was all too clear to her heart.

"Oh, Grant, darling, I love you."

It was utterly and absolutely the wrong thing to have said. Now he would feel that she was trying to push him into something they had already agreed could never happen.

No commitments. No strings. No happily-ever-after.

She accepted that. She *did*. It was just that she was... She was grateful to him, that's all. Grateful to him for being the one to unlock the mysteries of her body, for showing her what amazing depths of passion she was capable of. What woman wouldn't be grateful? What woman wouldn't be full of tender, loving feelings for the man who had done that? It didn't necessarily mean you were in love, though, she told herself sternly. But in her heart she knew she lied. Because she was in love with Grant Saxon. Desperately in love.

But how did she keep him from knowing it?

She wriggled sideways, sliding down to cuddle against his side as she had all the other times they'd made love over the past couple of days. She kissed his shoulder softly as if this time were no different, half of her hoping that he would simply assume her words had been spoken in the heat of passion and thus meant nothing; the other half praying that he'd realize how real they were and say them back to her. "G'night," she murmured, pretending a sleepiness she didn't feel in the least.

Automatically Grant's arm tightened around her, and he pressed a kiss to her hair. "G'night," he whispered, pretending, too.

They closed their eyes, both of them feigning sleep that was a long time in coming, lying there skin-to-skin with their minds miles apart on nearly parallel tracks.

I should never have pushed her into this, Grant was telling himself. *I knew from the beginning that she wasn't the kind of woman who could deal with a no-strings affair.*

I should never have thrown myself at him like that, Lily thought. *I knew he wasn't the kind of man who'd stick around for more than a few days.*

She'll be hurt, Grant berated himself.

He'll feel pressured, Lily reproached herself.

I should have had more self-control, they both thought in the last minutes before sleep finally claimed them.

The next morning, by unspoken mutual consent, they agreed to break camp and go back to the lodge instead of stretching out their time together as far as it would go.

"I have to get things ready for the kids," Lily said, although there was nothing she could think of that needed doing. "They'll be back this afternoon—the bus'll be in around two—and they have school tomorrow. I really should bake some cookies for their lunches next week and make sure they've got clean clothes and . . . things."

"Yeah," Grant agreed, beginning to dismantle the tent as he spoke. "I really need to put a few more facts together before I leave tomorrow."

Lily's eyes widened. "Tomorrow?" she said, trying to keep her voice from quavering. He was leaving tomorrow! "When?"

"Early. Real early." The sooner the better. "I want to get back to San Francisco before dark. And in this weather. . ." He shrugged.

She nodded, keeping her head down as she rearranged the contents of the ice chest. "Stop by the lodge before you leave and I'll fix you a packed lunch."

"You don't have to do that."

"It's all right. I want to." It was the last meal she would ever make for him, she thought despairingly. The last time she would see his face. The last— She sniffed determinedly and looked up from her kneeling position, a bright, false smile on her lovely face. "It wouldn't feel right to send you away hungry."

That smile twisted Grant's heart. *She's hurting already, dammit to hell!* And there was nothing he could do about it. Nothing except stay. And he couldn't do that. It wouldn't be good for either of them in the long run. "You're sure you want to?" he asked, because he didn't know what else to say. "It won't be any trouble?"

"No trouble," she said softly. "I'll fix it tonight when I make the kids' lunches. All you'll have to do is pick it up before you leave."

They finished packing up in silence, Lily raking through the campfire ashes to make sure they were well and thoroughly out. Grant loaded the tent and sleeping bag and ice chest into the rear of the Blazer for the short trip back to the lodge.

"Well, I guess I'd better get to work," Grant said when they'd stacked the camping equipment in a pile on the utility-room floor.

"Yes," Lily agreed. "I guess you'd better. I'd better, too. I've got lots to do before I go pick up the kids at the bus station." She opened the door to the kitchen.

He stopped her with a hand on her arm. "Lily?"

"Yes?"

"Lily, it's been . . ."

Oh, God, don't say fun, she thought. *Please don't say it's been fun.*

"It's been wonderful," he said at last, unable to think of another word that came close to what it had been without saying what it really was. *Dammit, Saxon, you're supposed to be the word merchant,* he thought irritably. *It was a hundred times more than wonderful. Tell her!* But he couldn't.

"Yes, it was wonderful," Lily agreed. *You made it wonderful.*

They stood there looking at each other for another endless second or two. Something more needed to be said, but neither of them knew what it was.

"Well," Lily said. "I'd better go in. All the heat's rushing out of the kitchen."

"Yes."

"Don't forget to stop by in the morning for your lunch."

"I won't." *Let her go*, he told himself. *Just let her go.*
He dropped his hand from her arm and turned away.

Lily stood just inside the back door of the lodge,
blinking back tears as he crossed the wintry yard and
disappeared into the front door of his cabin. Then her
tears welled up and over her lower lids, tracking silently down her pink, snow-kissed cheeks as she ran
inside and threw herself across the quilted spread on her
bed.

Thirty minutes later she stood at her bathroom sink,
splashing cold water on her face and telling herself in
no uncertain terms to straighten up.

."It's not the end of the world, Lily Talbot," she told
her reflection sternly, staring at the tear-streaked face
that looked back at her. "It only feels like it."

With quiet determination, she opened her medicine
chest and pulled out a few seldom-used cosmetics.
Carefully she began the painstaking process of cam-
ouflaging the redness around her eyes and nose. "Can't
let the kids see me like this," she mumbled to the mirror, patting foundation makeup over her eyelids. "It
would scare them to death."

Finally, satisfied that they would see nothing un-
usual when they looked at her, Lily brushed her hair
and glossed her lips and went, dry-eyed, to the kitchen
to make cookies for their homecoming. Six dozen
chocolate-chip cookies later, it was time to go pick them
up at the bus station.

"Mommy, Mommy! We're home! Look what I got!"
Elizabeth was the first off the bus. Flying down the steps
she threw herself into her mother's waiting arms. Lily

held her warm, wriggling little body as close as she could, burying her face in her daughter's soft blond curls.

Elizabeth tolerated the embrace for just a second. "Mommy, you're holding me too tight," she protested after a moment. "You're crushing my Thanksgiving turkey."

"Oh." Lily loosened her hold on the child. "I'm sorry, honey. I'm just so glad to have you home." She looked up as her two sons clambered off the bus. "All of you," she said, reaching out her hands to the boys, pulling them close for a kiss on the cheek. "I missed you all so much."

"But don' you want to see my turkey?" Elizabeth demanded.

"Yes, of course, Lizzie. Let me see your turkey. Oh, how pretty it is! Did you make this all by yourself?"

"Cynthia helped me a little," the child admitted.

"Were you a good girl for Cynthia?"

"No," said Sean before his sister could answer.

"I was, too!"

"Were not."

"Was—"

Lily barely heard the familiar argument as she herded them out to the Blazer. "Have we got all the luggage, Jeff?" she asked her elder son, smiling at him over the heads of the younger two. He was getting so tall; another year or two and he'd start putting on the weight to go with his height.

"Yeah," he said, loading it into the back of the car as everyone scrambled in. He climbed in the front seat beside his mother. "Are you okay, Mom?" he asked then, concern in the blue eyes that were so like hers.

"I'm fine, Jeff." She reached across the seat and squeezed his hand. "I just missed you kids so much this time. But now that you're all home, I'm fine." And she was, she told herself. She would be. Eventually. She would act fine for them, pretending that everything was okay the way she had after the divorce, and pretty soon it would be true. All it would take was time.

"Everybody buckled up?" she asked, turning the key in the ignition.

"Buckled," chorused three young voices in unison.

"Then we're off. Chocolate chip cookies and milk when we get home," she announced.

"Oh, boy!" said Sean. "Chocolate chip cookies! Cynthia doesn't make cookies."

"That's because she's preg'ant," Elizabeth said.

"Is not," Sean shot back, automatically disagreeing with his sister.

But Elizabeth wasn't interested in arguing just then. "Cynthia let me touch her stomach when the baby moved," she said. "Did I move inside your stomach, Mommy?"

"All the time." She smiled at her daughter in the rearview mirror, remembering the pleasure of carrying her. "I think you were practicing dancing in there."

Elizabeth giggled. "Did Sean move? An' Jeff?"

"Um-hmm. All of you kicked like the dickens."

"Did it hurt?"

"No. Sometimes it kept me awake at night, though."

"Do you like having babies?"

"I love having babies," Lily answered, wondering just what her daughter was leading up to.

"Then could you maybe have another baby pretty soon, Mommy, so we could have one down here and not have to go to Portlan' all the time to see Cynthia's?"

"Lizzie, you stupid." Sean popped his sister on the arm. "You have to be married to have babies."

Elizabeth glared at her brother. "Do you?" she demanded of her mother.

"Well, no, you don't *have* to be, but it usually works out better for everyone if you are," Lily answered honestly, wondering suddenly if that very question might be something she would have to cope with on a more personal basis in the near future.

She and Grant hadn't used anything that last time; in the searing heat of the moment, they'd both forgotten about contraception. And she got pregnant very, very easily. Was it the right time of the month, she wondered, trying to calculate it in her mind. Did she want it to be? And if it were, would she tell him? If she did, would he stand by her?

"Hey, Mom. Mom," Sean interrupted her reverie. "Can we go sledding after we have our cookies, huh? Could we?"

"Sledding? I don't know—"

"Yeah, Mom," Jeff said, seconding his younger brother's idea. "Just for a little while? It'd be fun."

"Okay, sledding it is," she agreed, pulling into the driveway of Talbot's Family Resort. The exercise would do them all good, and it would give her something to

think about besides the fact that Grant was leaving tomorrow. "Take all your stuff into the house, change into
your snowsuits, grab some cookies and we'll go. But
hurry it up; it gets dark early."

"Can we ask Mr. Saxon to come, too?" Elizabeth
asked, bouncing out of the car.

"No, you cannot ask Mr. Saxon. He's busy."

"No, he's not," Elizabeth persisted. "I can see him,
standing there at his window, watching us like he wants
to come sledding, too." She waved across the yard to
cabin four.

Lily grabbed her hand and pulled it down to her side.
"Mr. Saxon doesn't want to go sledding, Elizabeth. He's
busy."

"But—"

"No buts, young lady. Now, in the house and change
if you're coming with us."

Recognizing her mother's tone of voice, Elizabeth
stopped arguing and hurried inside after her brothers.
Lily lingered for a moment, telling herself that it was
only to gather up the paper turkey, the green knit muffler and the one reindeer-patterned mitten that her
children had left behind. She turned her head and
looked toward cabin four.

Grant was standing exactly where her daughter had
said he was. At the window, looking at her. From across
the width of the yard, through the veil of gently falling
snow, his expression appeared almost wistful, but she
couldn't tell for sure. He had a cup of coffee in his right
hand and something else—a sheaf of papers, perhaps—in his left. And he simply stood there, staring at

her staring at him. Neither of them moved or spoke or changed expression for a long moment, and then Lily turned, finally, and went into the lodge to hurry her children along.

THERE WERE HORDES of people on the sledding hill and the mood was merry; four days of steady snow had put enough powder down to make good sledding for the first time that year, and lots of families were out taking advantage of it.

Elizabeth and Sean tumbled out of the Blazer like excited puppies, laughing and yelling out greetings to their friends as Jeff and Lily unloaded the sleds.

"Mommy, there's Gina!" Elizabeth shouted, spotting her best friend. "Hey, Gina!" She went sprinting off up the hill.

"Lizzie, your cap!" Lily called, chasing after her daughter to pull the fuzzy knit cap over her head. "Now be careful," she warned, knotting the child's scarf more securely around her neck. She did the same to Sean. "See that your sister doesn't try anything fancy, okay?"

Sean nodded, impatient to join the excitement on the hill.

"Go on," she said, sending them off with a wave of her hand. She turned to her elder son as the other two scampered off, dragging the sled behind them. "Aren't you going with them?"

"Yeah," he said, but he made no move to follow his younger brother and sister. He fidgeted beside his mother instead, pulling at the fringed end of his striped muffler.

"Something on your mind, Jeff?" she said gently, knowing he needed prodding to bring up whatever was bothering him. Was he still worried about "that Mr. Saxon getting ideas" about his mother? Or, God forbid, had she somehow given away the fact that those "ideas" hadn't all been Grant Saxon's. "Jeff?"

"I talked to Dad while we were up there," he began, staring at the ground. "You know, about you and, ah, Mr. Saxon." He flashed a quick glance at his mother's face to see how she was taking it.

About Grant and me? What about Grant and me? "Yes?" she said evenly, keeping calm by sheer force of will. Good Lord, she thought, what did her son suspect? Or know? Was he old enough to know or guess about the things that she and Grant had been doing in the woods?

"Well, Dad said that, um, you had been alone a long time and that, ah . . ." He pulled a long loose thread out of his muffler and dropped it onto the snow, watching it as it fell. "That if you had found someone special, that I shouldn't make things hard for you by acting like I did after the divorce. He said I shouldn't let Lizzie or Sean make things hard for you, either. So, ah, we talked about it on the bus on the way home—me and Sean and Lizzie. They already like him. Mr. Saxon, I mean. So—" he looked at her squarely in the eyes, his fair skin flushed with adolescent embarrassment at discussing such an intimate subject with his mother "—if you want to date Mr. Saxon or . . . or marry him or something, well, I'll try to like him, too."

Lily felt her heart crinkle with love. "Oh, Jeff, honey, I love you," she said, wrapping her arms around him.

Jeff returned her embrace with a quick, hard squeeze. "Are you going to marry him?"

"No, Jeff, I'm not," she said firmly.

"It's not because of me, is it?" he asked worriedly, drawing away. "Because I was giving you a hard time? I won't anymore."

"You weren't giving me a hard time, Jeff. Don't think that."

"But if you're not gonna marry him . . . ?"

She put her hand on his cheek. "Mr. Saxon and I are just friends."

"But you *like* him, Mom. You like him a lot. I can tell. You look at him just like Dad looks at Cynthia."

Lily shook her head. When had her thirteen-year-old son become so perceptive? So sensitive to adult emotions? "We're just friends, honey. And that's all. Honest."

Jeff still looked doubtful.

"Grant's going back to San Francisco tomorrow morning," she told him.

"Is he coming back?"

Lily shook her head again, fighting the tears that were suddenly far too close to the surface. "No."

"Maybe if I talk to him. You know, man-to-man, and tell him that it's okay with Sean and Lizzie and me?"

"No, honey, really. It isn't necessary."

"But you're *crying*."

"Only a tiny bit, because I love you so much. And you're growing up so fast, right before my eyes." She smiled and reached up, brushing the blond hair back from his forehead. "Why don't you join Sean and Lizzie on the hill? It'll be dark soon and you won't even have gotten in one run down the hill."

His blue eyes scanned her face. "Are you sure, Mom?"

"Positive." She made her smile wider. "Go on." She gestured toward the hill. "I think I see Beth up there with her brother." Beth was a redheaded seventh-grader with shiny metal braces and the beginnings of what promised to be a spectacular figure. "Why don't you go on up and say hi?"

Still Jeff hesitated.

"Go," Lily ordered. "I have to go over and talk to Ruth Phelps, anyway." She gestured toward the small group of women clustered around the open tailgate of a station wagon. "Got to find out how many cakes to bake for the PTA Christmas bake sale."

Jeff waited until his mother had begun walking toward the station wagon, then turned and dashed up the hill.

TWILIGHT CAME and went, deepening into dusk and then full dark, and still Lily and the children hadn't returned. They'd gone sledding, Grant knew, because he'd watched them load the sleds into the back of the Blazer, all the while wishing that he was going with them. But they couldn't still be sledding in the dark. Could they?

No, they probably decided to go out to dinner, he told himself. But it was a school night. Lily wouldn't keep the kids up late on a school night.

So where the hell were they?

He began to worry.

Maybe one of the kids had gotten hurt and Lily had had to rush to the hospital for emergency care. A lot could go wrong when you were speeding down a hill on a sled. Half-buried rocks could send you tumbling through the air. You could crash into a tree. Fingers could be stomped on, or cut.

Grant winced, picturing Lizzie's chubby little fingers being sliced open by the runners of a sled. And Lily... Lily turned green at the sight of blood. She couldn't handle it alone, he thought, forgetting that she had been handling it alone for the past three years—and that, at least as far as he was concerned, she was going to be handling it alone for some time to come.

He grabbed his down jacket off the bed and headed for the door, intent only on going to her. Helping her.

But going where?

All he knew was that they had gone sledding.

He stopped for a minute with his hand on the doorknob, thinking. Vaguely he remembered seeing a likely-looking sledding hill not far from the lodge, just a few miles down the road. There'd been a small parking lot and, if he wasn't mistaken, a couple of brick fireplaces off to one side for picnicking and such. He'd drive there first, he decided, just to make sure everything was all right. And if they weren't there, he'd... well, he'd decide what to do if they weren't there.

Ten minutes later Grant turned into the small parking lot at the base of the sledding hill. Lily's white Blazer was still there, as were several other cars. A group of people were milling around in a rather disorganized way, the headlights of a car shining on them to provide illumination. Several more lights—lanterns and flashlights from the look of them—bobbed in and out among the trees surrounding the cleared area. Grant recognized the car with its headlights on as a police car.

What in the hell was going on?

"Lily?" he called, advancing on the group at a near run, "Lily, are you all right?"

She looked up at his voice. Her face was stark white. Her eyes were huge and dark in her pale face. "Grant." She turned away from the policeman who was questioning her and ran straight into his arms. "Oh, Grant. I'm so glad you're here. Sean's missing."

10

"How?" Grant said, grasping Lily's elbows to support her as she sagged against him. "When?"

"I don't know. I don't know." Her voice was high and thin, like a frightened child's. Her eyes were wide, glittering with unshed tears. He could feel her fingers digging into the flesh of his upper arms even through the heavy jacket he wore. "He was there one minute, sledding down the hill with his friends, and then he just wasn't. He didn't come when I called. I thought he was hiding at first, just playing a game because he didn't want to go home but *he's not here!*" Hysteria hovered on the edge, waiting. Lily closed her eyes, fighting for control, her lips pressed tight to still their trembling. She couldn't let herself fall apart. Sean needed her. And Jeff and Lizzie were already frightened enough without seeing their mother come unglued in front of them.

"Are you going to be all right?" Grant's voice, low and concerned, was right next to her ear.

She nodded her head. "Yes," she said, opening her eyes. She looked up at him, determination not to fall apart etched in every line of her face. She squeezed his biceps once more, hard, as if drawing strength from him, then dropped her hands. "Yes, I'll be fine." She reached out and touched her children, gathering them to her. "We'll all be fine."

"M-Mommy, I'm scared," Lizzie said, letting go of her brother's hand to grasp her mother's. Her little face was tear-streaked, her lips quivering. "I'm scared. Is Sean gonna die?"

Lily swooped down and scooped the child up in her arms. "No, Lizzie, no! He's just lost, that's all. We'll find him." She pressed her daughter's head to her shoulder. "We'll find him," she murmured. She looked up at Grant, seeking reassurance as she said it.

He reached out and covered Lily's hand, cupping Lizzie's head as he did so. Without thinking, his other hand touched Jeff's shoulder. The boy stiffened but didn't move away. "Yes, we'll find him," he said. "Don't worry."

"Mr. Talbot?" The young policeman who had been questioning Lily spoke diffidently, hating to interrupt what looked like a private family moment.

Grant shook his head. "I'm a friend of the family," he said, pulling Lily—and Elizabeth—into the curve of his arm, keeping his hand on Jeff's shoulder. "Name's Saxon. Grant Saxon. What is it?"

"There's no use searching anymore tonight, sir. It's too—"

"Not search!" Lily shifted out of Grant's embrace, rounding on the young officer like a mother tiger, Lizzie still held protectively in her arms. "You have to search! My son's lost out there somewhere. He's only ten years old. Just a little boy and—" She turned to Grant, her eyes frantic. "Tell him they can't stop searching!"

"Mrs. Talbot, it's full dark. The searchers are just stumbling around out—"

Grant cut him off with a slash of his hand. "How long has Sean been missing, Lily? When was the last time you saw him?"

"Forty, maybe forty-five, minutes ago. He was sharing a toboggan with the Phelps boys. They were pulling it up the hill together."

"Jeff?"

The teenager answered him steadily. "About the same, I think, maybe a little less. I was with Beth at the top of the hill and we stopped to watch them go down on the toboggan because we thought it was gonna crash. They had six or seven kids piled on it," he explained. "But it got to the bottom all right. So me and Beth went down together on my sled."

Grant looked at the police officer. "Forty-five minutes at most," he said. "Probably less. He can't have gotten very far."

"Far enough not to hear us calling him, sir. We even blasted the siren a few times but there was no answer. Look," he said sympathetically, "I know this is hard, but there's nothing anyone can do in the dark. All those people are accomplishing out there now—" he waved a hand toward the lights bobbing through the trees "—is to thoroughly obliterate any trail that he might have left."

"Dogs?" Grant demanded.

"Yes, sir, but with all the confusion they can't pick up any individual trail." He shook his head regretfully. "The best thing to do is call a halt now and start searching again in the morning."

"But he's just a little boy!" Lily cried. "He'll be cold and afraid and—"

Elizabeth began to weep noisily.

"If you won't look for my brother, I will!" Jeff exploded, twisting out from under Grant's hand.

"No, you can't." Lily reached out and grabbed his jacket with one hand, clutching Lizzie to her with the other. "I will not have both my sons lost out there in the woods. Jeff, come back here. I— Grant, stop him!"

"Jeff!" The word cracked through the air like a whip, halting the boy in his tracks. "Your mother said no."

Jeff whirled around. "But he's my brother!" Tears stood in his eyes.

"I know, Son." The word slipped out without either of them being aware of it. "I know. But your getting lost too isn't going to help him any."

"I won't get lost," Jeff argued. "I know how to find my way in the woods, about snow survival and stuff. Tim's on the ski patrol and he taught us how to—"

"Tim taught you snow survival?" Grant interrupted, thinking, *Finally, a piece of good news in all this!* "Sean, too?"

Jeff nodded. "He's been on campouts with the Scouts in wintertime, too. They teach all the kids what to do if they get lost, how to dig snow shelters and stuff," he added, beginning to see what Grant was getting at. "Sean got his merit badge, no sweat."

Grant looked at Lily, his eyes serious as he told her what he must. "Then I think the officer's right," he said softly. "We should wait until morning when we can all see what we're doing."

"But Grant . . ." Lily's voice quavered and nearly broke. Her son was out there somewhere, alone, and the man she loved was telling her to leave him out there all night.

"He's dressed warmly isn't he?" Grant reminded her. "Ski suit, moon boots, mittens, hat?"

Lily nodded, sudden hope springing up. Yes, Sean was dressed warmly. His ski suit was insulated with synthetic down. He was wearing thermal underwear, two pairs of socks and a turtleneck sweater. He wouldn't freeze, even on a colder night than this one promised to be.

"If he knows any snow survival at all, then he knows to dig himself a shelter and wait for help to come." He looked at Jeff. "Would he do that?"

Jeff nodded eagerly. "Yes. Yes, he'd do that. Mom, he'd do that! It's exactly what Tim told us to do."

"Then he should be fine until morning," Grant said.

"But he'll be so afraid. And hungry," Lily objected. "He hasn't had dinner yet, just a couple of cookies and a glass of milk before we left the lodge. That's all."

Elizabeth lifted her head from Lily's neck. "Sean has cookies in his pocket," she said.

"What?" Both adults spoke at once.

"He put a whole bunch of cookies in his pockets when Mommy wasn't looking. Choc'late-chip cookies are Sean's most favorite."

"See there," Grant said, smoothing Lizzie's hair. "He's got everything he needs. He'll be fine." *Unless he's fallen and hurt himself. Unless he's lying unconscious somewhere.* But Grant didn't say any of what he was thinking to the three pairs of blue eyes that were looking up at him so trustingly.

"Do you really think so?" Lily said piteously, asking for reassurance.

"I really think so." He glanced sideways at the policeman still standing there. "Don't you agree, Officer?"

"Yes, sir, I do." The young man nodded. "I'll just get these people rounded up, tell them we're calling the search off for tonight."

"But you'll be back in the morning, first thing, won't you?"

"Yes, ma'am. We will. First light," he assured her.

"You get the kids in the car, Lily," Grant ordered gently, giving her a little push to get her moving. "Go back to the lodge. I want to have a few words with the officers first, find out exactly what their plans are for tomorrow morning. I'll just be a few minutes behind you. Go on."

"I'll come with you," Jeff said.

"Your mother needs you now," Grant reminded him.

Jeff started to object, then nodded and turned, herding his mother toward the Blazer with an arm around her shoulders. "Sean'll be all right, Mom," Grant heard him say. "You'll see. It's probably just like Mr. Saxon said. He's probably dug himself a really neat snow shelter. He'll be fine."

Please God, let that be the truth, Grant prayed, waiting as the police officers rounded up all the would-be rescuers and sent them home.

"Any indications that the boy didn't wander off by himself?" Grant asked when he got the two policemen alone.

"None that we've found, sir," one of them said. "Course, with all these people tramping all over hell and back, it's hard to tell anything for sure. But everything points to the kid just wandering off on his own the way kids are apt to do sometimes. Got farther away than he meant to and got lost."

"No signs that he might have been injured out there?" Grant jerked his head toward the trees.

"None that we've seen."

Grant nodded. There wasn't anything else to ask, because there could be no answers until Sean was found. "First light, then," he said wearily, putting out his hand to shake theirs.

"First light, sir." The two young policemen turned together toward their patrol car.

Grant headed into the woods.

It was just as the officer had said—footprints heading every which way, crisscrossing one another until there was no telling one set from the other. He stood very still in the darkness and listened. Listened for any slight noise, any cry that might now be audible in the muffled stillness of the snow-shrouded night.

Nothing.

Not a whisper of sound. Just the quietly falling snow, the low moan of the wind rustling through the pines, and the darkness.

Damn, he thought savagely, his fists clenched at his sides. *The poor little kid has to be scared to death out there by himself.* And he could do nothing about it. Grant had never felt so helpless, so utterly useless, in his entire life.

"Sean!" His voice rang out through the stillness, echoing through the trees.

There was no answer.

He went farther into the woods, pausing every few steps to stop and listen.

"Sean!"

Nothing.

Disheartened, he turned back toward the parking lot. As he came out of the trees he could see two vehicles. The Jeep he had rented—and Lily's Blazer. All three occupants were in the front seat, huddled close together for warmth and comfort. Lily rolled the window down as Grant approached.

"You were supposed to be on your way home," he chided gently.

"I know. But I couldn't." She looked toward the silent, foreboding darkness of the trees. "God, I hate to just leave him there! I keep thinking there must be something I can do." She blinked, holding the tears at bay by sheer force of will. "Something."

"You can be strong for Lizzie and Jeff," he said, telling her what she already knew. "They need you to be strong right now." He reached into the open window and cupped her cheek. "He'll be all right, Lily," he reassured her softly, his thumb brushing at the dampness under her eyes. "He's a tough little nut."

"I know."

Grant withdrew his hand. "Start her up," he instructed. "I'll follow you home."

THE HOURS OF THE NIGHT were long, some of the longest that Grant had ever spent. It nearly broke his heart to watch Lily try to pretend that she wasn't almost out of her mind with worry about her middle child.

She busied herself in the kitchen first, keeping Jeff and Elizabeth close to her while she made them a dinner of grilled cheese sandwiches and soup. Cream of mushroom soup because it was Sean's least favorite and it made her feel better somehow to be fixing something that her youngest son wouldn't be sorry to have missed out on.

"Sean don't like mushroom soup," Elizabeth informed the room at large, listlessly stirring it with a spoon. "He likes choc'late chip cookies better."

"Yeah, he'll be glad he missed it," Jeff added, trying manfully to cheer his silent, unsmiling mother. He looked across the table and smiled at his little sister, trying to lift her spirits, too. "Hey, Lizzie, tomorrow let's tell him we had chicken noodle instead." Chicken noodle was Sean's favorite. "It'll serve him right for taking all those chocolate chip cookies."

His ploy worked, earning him an approving glance from Grant as Elizabeth brightened at the thought of taking revenge on her adored nemesis.

"An' let's tell him we had hamburgers, too, instead of cheese sam'iches. No, no, let's tell him we went to McDonald's!" she said, looking to her mother for confirmation. "He won't never get losted again if he has to miss McDonald's," she said, looking to her mother for confirmation. "Will he, Mommy?"

"No," Lily answered softly, summoning up a smile for her daughter. "He sure won't."

"I know I wouldn't," Grant said then, picking up the ball before it could drop. "Those chocolate shakes are my favorite." He bit into his grilled cheese sandwich with every evidence of enjoyment, although eating was the last thing he felt like doing at the moment. Not while there was a little boy out there in the night with only a pocketful of cookies for his dinner. But if the little boy's mother could hold back her fear for the sake of her other two children, then so could he. "What's your favorite, Lizzie?"

She thought a moment before answering. "Everything," she said. Then, "Sean likes the french fries best. With lots an' lots of catsup. Once he got a whole bunch of those little catsup thingies when Mommy wasn't looking—fifty, at least, I think," she exaggerated innocently. "An' he put them in his pockets. An' he forgot about them for a long time an' then he sat on them an' they went *squish!* all over the chair. It was so funny."

"Oh, yeah, I remember," chimed in Jeff, laughing at the memory. "It looked like he'd been shot in the butt."

Lily laughed, too, but inside she was crying. They were talking about him the way people did about the deceased at a funeral reception. The way people did about someone who was terminally ill. Logically she knew it was only their way of keeping Sean in their midst until they had him back for real, a way of keeping their fears at bay. But it made her want to scream.

Her hands clenched on the dish towel she held as if by squeezing hard enough she could hold back the need to go running into the night to look for him. It wouldn't do any good, she knew. It would only make things worse. But it was hard, so hard, to stay inside—warm and dry and fed—and do nothing while her child faced the unknown terrors of the cold, dark night alone.

Grant's hand covered hers on the towel, gently pulling it from her grasp, and she realized that she must have been standing at the sink for several minutes, staring into the nothingness in her mind.

"Why don't we all go into the living room, Lily?" Grant said softly. "Turn on the TV or play cards or—"

She looked at him with soft, incredulous eyes. "Play cards?"

It sounded ludicrous hearing it repeated back like that. *Play cards while Sean is lost out in the woods?* she seemed to say. Hell, it was ludicrous. But what was the alternative? He couldn't just let her stand there, staring silently into the night, torturing herself with crazy imaginings until it got light enough to go look for her son.

"Come on into the living room, Lily," he said again. His voice was low, for her ears only. "You're scaring the kids silly."

She shifted her glance to the table. He was right. Jeff and Lizzie were watching her, their halting smiles gone, fear and uncertainty on both young faces.

"Mom?" Jeff said.

"Mommy?"

She took a deep breath and pulled herself together. She could do nothing to make tonight easier for Sean. But she could make things easier for Jeff and Lizzie. "Grant's right," she said with a smile, holding her hands out to them. "Let's go into the living room and get comfortable. I'll read to you until it's time for bed."

They settled onto the sofa, each of them unconsciously craving the reassurance of touch. Lily sat in the middle with Lizzie and a book in her lap; Jeff sat on one

side, his head resting against her shoulder; Grant settled on her other side, his arm curved behind her on the
sofa back. Lily began to read to them from a book of
Aesop's fables, her voice low and steady and reassuring in the otherwise silent room.

Bedtime came and went for each child but no one
suggested that they be bundled off to their separate
rooms. Unnoticed and unheard, the clock in the hall-
way chimed each hour as it slipped by in slow motion.
The snow continued to drift past the long windows on
either side of the fireplace. And the pages rustled beneath Lily's fingers as one story was finished and another begun.

Elizabeth tumbled into unwilling sleep, finally, and
then Jeff followed her, his head sagging against his
mother's shoulder. And still Lily read, keeping the de-
mons at bay in the only way she could.

Grant rose then, silently, to feed the fire and follow
his nose to a bedroom for blankets to cover the sleeping children. Gently he moved them to more comfortable positions, shifting Jeff so his head rested against the
armrest instead of his mother's shoulder, taking the
dead weight of six-year-old Elizabeth from Lily's arms
to lay her against the other armrest.

Without a word he eased the book from Lily's hands,
closed it and laid it on the coffee table. Pulling her to
her feet, he backed into the big overstuffed chair that
sat at right angles to the sofa, sat down and took her
onto his lap. She curled into his arms like a tired child
seeking comfort.

He cradled her against him as if she were exactly that. "You should try to get some sleep, too," he whispered against her hair.

"I can't. If I close my eyes I can see Sean out there...somewhere. Alone in the dark. He's afraid and cold and—"

Grant's arms tightened around her. "Don't, Lily." He pressed his lips to the crown of her head. "Don't torture yourself like that. He'll be fine."

"But he's so little, Grant." She shifted in his lap to look at him. "Just a baby, really. He shouldn't be out by himself at night. He—"

"Lily, stop it!" he whispered fiercely, rage at his helplessness ripping through him at the pain and fear in her eyes. Pain he was unable to do anything about, fear that he was unable to alleviate. "Stop it right now before you make yourself crazy!" He put his hand to her head, pressing her face into his neck much as she had done to Elizabeth earlier. "You've done great so far, sweetheart. You've done what had to be done with hardly a whimper. You've been strong," he crooned, soothing her. "A rock for Jeff and Lizzie."

And she had, he realized. As soon as she had been made to see that nothing could be done for Sean tonight, she had fought down her own mounting terror to do what she could for the two children who needed her. She might turn green at the sight of blood, might be charmingly unable to cope with her own stubbed toe, but give her a real emergency to face, other people to consider, and she became a tower of strength. A woman any man would be proud to call his own.

"Be strong a little longer, love. Just a little longer. It'll be light soon."

She nodded, her tousled blond hair brushing softly against his cheek. "I'm glad you're here, Grant."

"So am I," he whispered into her hair, meaning it. "So am I."

She made a little nestling movement and seemed to relax in his arms. "I think I'll make blueberry pancakes for breakfast," she said quietly after a moment. "I still have a couple of pints that I froze last summer. All three of the kids love them but Sean especially. And especially with warm blueberry syrup. He'd put blueberry syrup on cornflakes if I'd let him." He felt her smile against his neck at the thought. "That child has the strangest tastes in food."

She went on talking quietly, reflectively, telling him little stories about Sean until, finally, her voice drifted off and she fell into an uneasy sleep. He continued to sit, brushing her hair back from her cheek with an easy rhythmic motion that soothed them both, staring into the fire until he fell into a doze himself. He woke a short while later to the sound of his name, opening his eyes to see Jeff staring at him from his place on the sofa. For just a moment, Grant felt a start of guilt at being caught with Lily in his arms, but it eased almost instantly. It wasn't necessary to feel guilty; Jeff was no longer jealous.

The boy's eyes flickered toward the window, a question in his glance. Not quite first light but almost.

Grant nodded and gently roused the woman in his arms.

She came awake instantly. "Is it time? Can we go look for him?"

"Shh," Grant warned, tilting his head toward the still-sleeping Elizabeth. "Yes, it's time. But 'we' aren't going to look for him, I am."

"And me," Jeff said softly but very firmly, throwing back the blanket as he sat up.

"And Jeff," Grant acknowledged, setting Lily on her feet as he stood up.

"But I—"

Grant put his finger over his lips and glanced at Elizabeth again. The child lay sprawled on her back with the blanket twisted around her, sleeping the sleep of the utterly exhausted. "She shouldn't have to wake up and go out in the cold again," Grant said. "Neither should you."

"I want to find my son!" Lily's voice was low but fierce.

"We'll find him for you," he promised. "No—" He touched his finger to her lips, stopping her. "You stay here and start breakfast. I—" He glanced over at her elder son. "Jeff and I," he corrected, "will have him back in time to eat a dozen of your blueberry pancakes hot off the griddle."

She hesitated, her eyes darting from the sleeping Elizabeth to the snow outside the window and back again, weighing the needs of one child against the other.

Grant took her hands in both of his. "I promise, Lily," he said solemnly. "I'll bring him back to you in time for breakfast."

She squeezed his hands. "All right. Go. But hurry. Please hurry."

11

GRANT AND JEFF arrived at the sledding hill just minutes before the rescue squad did. And they were across the parking lot and into the snow-shrouded trees before the group of professionals had time to get out of their cars, get organized and disperse. But Grant's haste was fueled not by civic responsibility or the prospect of a job to do or even the thought of Sean's probable discomfort, but by Lily's frightened blue eyes looking up into his so trustingly, so full of the belief that he could make things right. He had to bring her son back to her. And quickly.

"He can't have gone too far," he said to Jeff, thinking aloud as they melted into the trees. "It was already starting to get dark when he turned up missing, and it was pitch-dark by the time the search was called off. He'd have started bumping into things before long and would've had to stop."

"But he didn't see all the lights when we were looking for him. He didn't hear us calling him," Jeff pointed out. "He didn't even hear the police siren. And they blasted it a couple times. He'd have to be pretty far away not to hear that."

Or have been knocked unconscious by butting heads with a tree in the dark, Grant thought, but he didn't say it. He came to a halt, looking around for some kind of sign, any sign, which way Sean might have gone.

The crisscrossing footprints were still everywhere, half obscured now by the snow that had fallen during the night. Any trail that might have led them to Sean had been all but obliterated by the people that had tramped around the night before.

"Head over that way," he directed Jeff. "Look for any set of footprints that leads away from all this mess here. But don't get out of sight." He smiled at the teenager, a travesty of his usual lighthearted grin. "Your mother'd skin me alive if you turned up missing, too," he said, not doubting it for a minute.

Jeff nodded and managed to grin back at him.

"I'll work around this way. Call his name at about sixty-second intervals. Give him enough time to hear you and holler back. Okay?"

"Okay." Jeff started walking, head down, studying the snow-covered ground for a sign. "Sean!" he bellowed, pausing for a moment to listen for an answer. The name echoed back on the still, morning air. "Sean!"

A minute passed, and then another and another, the only sounds their own two voices calling out at the prescribed intervals and the squeaky crunch of new snow under their boots as they moved farther away from the sledding area.

How could he have gotten this far, Grant wondered, all alone and in the dark? Then, Dammit, weren't little kids supposed to be afraid of going off in the dark by themselves? Was he going to be able to keep his promise to Lily? Could he bring her son back for breakfast and all in one piece?

"Here! Mr. Saxon, here!" Jeff called excitedly. "I think I've found his trail!"

A single pair of footprints, too small for a grown man, veered off from the rest, heading deeper into the woods.

"That's him," Grant said, praying it was true. "It's got to be."

They took off at a trot, following the hazy, half-hidden trail of footprints, oblivious to the sounds of the rescue team who had entered the woods behind them.

"Sean!" Jeff's clear young voice rang out. "Sean, where are you?"

"Sean!" Grant's deeper baritone rumble echoed through the woods.

"Here!" The voice was muffled and faint. "I'm right here."

They came to a dead stop, listening, heads cocked like hunting dogs. "Where?" they said at almost the same time.

"Here." There was a rustling in the trees ahead, a soft *plop* as snow was dislodged from the branches, and then a flash of brilliant kelly green as a stocking-capped head poked out from beneath the low-hanging limbs of a stately snow-covered pine. "I'm right here." The face beneath the cap was rosy, the blue eyes as bright as they had been the time he'd peeked around Grant's cabin door, the smile one of welcome and relief. "Hi, you guys."

Grant felt a surge of relief so intense that it almost knocked him over. *Alive!* he exalted silently, not admitting until this moment that he had ever, for even the tiniest second, thought otherwise. Sean was alive and unhurt. He had kept his promise to Lily.

He rushed over, outdistancing Jeff with his longer stride, and pulled Sean from under the tree before he could crawl the rest of the way out on his own.

"Are you all right?" he demanded, setting the boy on his feet. "Everything work okay? Any frostbite?" he said, yanking off Sean's knit gloves to check for himself. The boy's hands were toasty warm. Grant touched his cheek with the backs of his fingers. Warm, too. The flush was not from the cold; rather it was the rosy glow of a child who had just awakened from a sound sleep.

Sleep, Grant thought incredulously, staring down at the boy. *The kid has been sleeping like a baby while we were all out of our minds with worry!* He didn't know whether to hug the little twerp until he popped or beat the living daylights out of him for scaring them all half to death.

Jeff suffered from no such dilemma. "Mom's gonna *kill* you!" he said furiously, pushing his younger brother hard enough to topple him backward into the snow. "But I'm gonna kill you first!"

"What'd I do?" Sean demanded, glaring up at his brother from his seat in the snow. "I didn't do anything!"

"Didn't do anything? You call running off just when we're supposed to go home not doing anything?" Jeff demanded indignantly. "Mom's been worried sick. She's been practically *crying* because of you. Lizzie's been crying." The tips of his ears were red with anger. His body was shaking. "The *police* have been looking for you."

"I didn't do it on purpose," Sean defended himself.

"Yeah, tell that to Mom!" Jeff yelled, launching himself at Sean. The two boys collided with a muffled *oof*, punching each other through their layers of cold-weather clothing.

Grant went down on one knee, grabbing a handful of each jacket. "That's enough, fellas," he said, pulling them apart. "Enough."

"He made Mom cry," Jeff exploded, breathing hard from exertion and the sudden release of fear for his brother. He twisted in Grant's grasp, trying to land another punch.

"I didn't mean to," Sean defended himself, his lips quivering even as he continued to swing at his brother. "I just saw some rabbit tracks and followed 'em, that's all. I didn't mean to get lost." He kicked out, aiming at his brother's shins.

Grant shook them once, hard. "Stop it!" he roared. Then, suddenly, without any of them quite knowing how it had happened, the two boys found themselves wrapped in Grant's strong arms in a three-way hug, all of them struggling manfully against tears of relief and emotion.

That was when the flashbulb went off.

"What the hell?" Grant lifted his head, blinking in the direction of the light.

Another bulb flashed. "That'll make a great front page," someone said. "'Lost boy returned to family.' Great human-interest stuff."

Grant rose to his feet, one of Lily's sons under his arm on either side of him, a question in his eyes.

"Local press," the photographer answered, giving the name of his paper. "Name's Harrison. This is Wheeler." He jerked his thumb toward a woman with a notepad and pen at the ready. "She'd like to ask the kid a few questions."

"In a minute," Grant said, turning his attention to the two police officers he'd met last night. "As you can see, we've found him."

"Everything okay? We have a paramedic on hand if he needs one."

Grant shook his head. "Thanks, but he's fine," he said, starting the whole group moving toward the parking lot. "None the worse for wear. Can't say the same for myself, though," he added, his smile wry and self-deprecating.

The reporter fell into step beside them. "I'm Kay Wheeler," she introduced herself to Grant. "We heard on the police scanner about your son being lost," she said, and then turned her attention to Sean, not giving Grant a chance to correct her assumption. "You must be—" a quick look at her notes "—Sean Talbot," she said, smiling at the boy. "Heard you had a scary night."

"Naw."

"You weren't scared out here all by yourself?" she coaxed. "Not even a little bit?"

Sean shrugged. "Maybe a little," he admitted.

"How'd you keep warm?"

"In there." Sean pointed back at the tree he had taken refuge under. "I crawled under the tree and dug down in the snow a little bit."

"And that kept you warm?"

"Uh-huh."

"Bet you got hungry, though."

Sean shrugged again. "Naw."

"His pockets were full of cookies," Jeff said. "He swiped 'em before we came sledding."

"Cookies, huh." She scribbled into her notebook. "Is that why you ran away? You were in trouble over taking the cookies?"

"Huh?" Sean looked blank for a moment. "I didn't run away," he said indignantly. "I was tracking a rabbit."

"He was lost," Jeff explained.

"Lost?"

"Yes, Ms Wheeler. Lost," Grant said firmly, feeling an unaccustomed surge of . . . something. Protectiveness, he thought. The reporter was only doing her job but no one was going to imply that Sean had any reason to run away from home in *his* presence. "As in wandered too far away from the sledding hill and lost his bearings in the woods."

Ms Wheeler backed off immediately. "Can you tell me how it feels to have your son back safe and sound?" She said then. "I'll bet you and your wife are relieved."

"Yes, his mother will be very relieved," Grant answered, again not correcting her assumption—and not inquiring too closely into his reasons for not doing so. "As soon as she knows he *is* safe and sound. So if you'll excuse us . . ." He took Sean's hand in his, grasped Jeff's shoulder and headed for the car. "Come on, boys, we've got hot blueberry pancakes waiting for us at home."

LILY CAME RUNNING OUT into the yard to meet them, the tears she had not allowed herself to shed during the long night falling freely at the sight of her son safe and sound.

Laughing, crying, she embraced Sean, then Jeff, then Sean again. "You found him! Oh, Grant, you found him!" She threw her arms around Grant for a quick, exuberant hug, then embraced her younger son again.

"Actually, Jeff found him," Grant said, trying to give credit where credit was due, but Lily wasn't listening. She was too busy assuring herself that everything was as it should be.

"Are you all right, Sean? Really all right?" she asked, holding him by the shoulders so that she could look at him. But even her keen mother's eye had to admit that he looked none the worse for wear—better than she did right then. There were no mauve circles of worry under Sean's blue eyes. She threw her arms around him again, hugging tight.

"I'm sorry I made you cry, Mom," Sean said against her breast, his arms equally tight around her. "I didn't mean to. I was just trying to track the rabbit, that's all. I didn't mean to make you cry."

"I know, darling. I know you didn't." She leaned away from him, holding his face between her hands. "And it's all right. You're back now. You're safe." She laughed softly, happily, and brushed back the hair on his forehead. "Just don't ever do that to me again or I'll lock you in your room until you're eighteen! You hear me?"

"I won't."

She ruffled his hair and let him go. "Good."

"Okay, everybody in the house," she ordered, wiping at her happy tears. She reached out to touch Jeff again as she made the demand, and then Grant, herding them all into the house in front of her.

"Get inside, Lizzie," she said to the little girl standing on the porch in her footed pajamas. "It's freezing out here."

They all trooped into the house as ordered, Lily still reaching out to touch and caress and reassure herself that all her loved ones were safe and well.

"Did you see any bears?" Elizabeth demanded eagerly, bouncing up and down in her excitement.

"Naw. I think I heard one, though. It came sniffing around the tree where I was."

"It was probably just a squirrel," Jeff scoffed.

"No, it was a bear," Sean said.

"A big bear?" Elizabeth asked, wide-eyed. "Was it a big bear, Sean?"

Lily's smile as she watched them was, Grant thought, like the sun coming up in the morning, giving warmth wherever it touched. She turned then, including him in its glow.

"Thank you, Grant," she whispered, going into his arms as naturally as if she did it every day of her life. She pressed her cheek to his heart, her arms sliding around his waist to hug him tight. "Thank you for bringing him back to me." Then, unconcerned that her children were in the same room, she went up on tiptoe and touched her mouth to his.

The kiss was warm and sweet and passionate and adoring. It said everything she felt. It went on almost forever. And it scared Grant Saxon—adventurer, loner, confirmed bachelor—to death.

Because everything that she was saying to him with her lips, he wanted to say right back. And he had never wanted to do that before in his life. Never wanted to say I love you, too. Never wanted to say I need you. Never *wanted* period, the way he wanted her. But dammit, he didn't want to want her. It didn't fit in with his plans.

"Are you going to marry Mommy?" Elizabeth's high, sweet voice pierced the silence of the room.

Grant stiffened at the words, denying to himself that they stirred him in any way—except to utter panic.

Lily sighed and lowered herself back to her heels. "No," she said, looking up at Grant as if the words were meant for him. "Mr. Saxon is not going to marry Mommy."

"Why not?" Elizabeth wanted to know. "You're kissing each other."

"Just because people kiss doesn't mean they're going to get married," Lily said, easing out of Grant's embrace.

"But—"

Jeff put his hand over his sister's mouth, stopping whatever she had been going to say next. "When's breakfast?"

"Just as soon as you boys get out of those damp clothes." Lily turned to the stove and flicked a switch under the griddle. "So you'd better hurry, both of you. You go on too, Lizzie," she said, before the little girl could object. "Go put a robe on before you catch a chill."

Silence filled the kitchen. Heavy, ponderous silence. Grant had no idea what to say. He felt as if he should apologize, but he wasn't quite sure what for. He wanted

to take her in his arms and kiss her senseless, but tha
would only make things worse. He wanted to stay with
her forever—and to run before the trap closed an
tighter around his neck.

"You should probably change, too," Lily said
reaching for a wooden spoon to stir the pancake batte
that didn't need stirring. "The knees of your jeans ar
all wet."

"Lily, I . . ."

"You have plenty of time before breakfast is ready.

"I'm not going to stay for breakfast."

Her hand stilled, just for a moment, and then sh
resumed stirring the batter. "Staying for breakfas
doesn't obligate you to anything, Grant," she sai
softly.

He said nothing. He didn't know what to say.

She turned and faced him. "Nothing that's hap
pened between us obligates you to anything at all. W
made that clear in the beginning, remember? N
strings. No commitments. Just because I broke tha
agreement by getting . . . getting emotionally involve
doesn't change anything."

"Lily, I'm sorry. I—"

She put up a hand, stopping him. "I'm not. We share
a wonderful, beautiful experience." She didn't say I lov
you, but they both knew that's what she meant. "Ho
could I be sorry about that?"

"I hurt you."

"Nothing that won't heal," she lied, trying to mal
it easier for him to do what he had to do. "So sto
looking so guilty, will you?"

"I *feel* guilty, dammit! I should have left you alone

"You didn't seduce some naive innocent," she said, almost exasperated with him. "Quite the contrary. I'm a grown woman with three children. I've been married and divorced. And it's not as if you didn't let me know from the very beginning what was what. *So stop feeling guilty.*" She turned back to the stove and took a deep, steadying breath. "How many pancakes would you like?"

"None. I'm not staying. I can't." If he stayed now, he was afraid that he would never leave.

She nodded and began pouring neat circles of pancake batter onto the hot griddle just as all three kids came back into the kitchen.

"Say goodbye to Mr. Saxon, kids," she said, forcing a bright note into her voice. "He has to get going."

"Already?"

"Right now?"

"But, Mommy, I wanted to show him my rocks."

"He has a long drive ahead of him, and it gets dark early this time of year. Not to mention the condition of the roads with all this snow." She looked directly at her youngest child. "You wouldn't want him to have an accident because he'd had to drive in the dark, would you?"

"No, but—"

"No buts. Say goodbye to Mr. Saxon." *Say goodbye, please, before I break down completely.*

"Goodbye, Mr. Saxon," Elizabeth said obediently. She came up to him, raising her face to be kissed. "Come back soon."

He bent down and brushed his lips across her baby-soft cheek, fighting the almost overwhelming urge to pick her up and nuzzle. "Bye, Lizzie. Be a good girl."

"I will," she promised.

"Goodbye, Mr. Saxon. Have a safe trip back." Jeff held out his hand.

"I think you're old enough to call me Grant," Grant said, shaking it. He turned to Sean. "Don't go wandering off into any more woods, okay?"

"Okay."

He looked longingly at the woman standing at the stove. "Goodbye, Lily. Take care of yourself."

She nodded. "You too," she said, smiling as if her heart wasn't, right this very minute, cracking clean down the middle. "Drive carefully."

It wasn't until later that she remembered that she hadn't fixed a lunch for him to take with him. Would he remember to stop for something nutritious on the way back to San Francisco, she wondered.

12

GRANT THREW his little black book down in disgust. *A through Z*, he thought, *and not one name interests me.* He had dated half a dozen women in the past month, even going so far as to try to rekindle the flame with Marcie, but nothing had happened. Absolutely nothing. Women who once would have had him howling at the moon were leaving him as cold as a week-old corpse.

And why? Because he kept comparing them all to one slender, soft-eyed divorcée with three kids. That was why, dammit! He had thought that once he'd gotten away from her, once he'd put several hundred miles and a week or two between himself and temptation, she would cease to invade his every waking thought. And his every sleeping one, too, if it came to that. But it hadn't worked out that way.

Instead he'd thought about her more.

He took a woman to brunch at a first-class restaurant—and thought about the pancake breakfast he'd had in Lily's old-fashioned kitchen. He escorted a high-fashion model in a barely-there piece of designer fluff to a holiday party—and thought about the way Lily looked in her worn blue jeans with the fuzzy leg-warmers that ran halfway up her thighs. He went to the symphony with an elegant socialite—and spent the evening daydreaming about sitting next to Lily in a darkened grade-school auditorium.

And when he'd tried to get passionate, well, the less said about that, the better, he thought. The look of surprise and passion on Lily's face when she melted in his arms was all that he could see when he thought about taking a woman to bed.

Dammit all to hell!

What did he see in her? he asked himself savagely. She wasn't his type. Not by a long shot. He'd always liked his women unencumbered and unencumbering, his relationships simple and fleeting. Lily Talbot was the antithesis of every woman he had ever been involved with. She was a mother hen, a homebody, a clinging vine; the kind of woman, he told himself, who would chain a man to her side and never let him go. . . .

Only he knew it wasn't true. She hadn't tried to chain him in any way. Not with promises or threats or tears. She hadn't pushed him to make a declaration he wasn't ready to make. She hadn't pushed him to do anything. She had just been her own sweet, warm, loving self— giving all, asking nothing.

Dammit, didn't she want *anything* from him?

"You're driving yourself crazy, Saxon," he said aloud. "Give it time."

But he'd already given it nearly a month, and it was getting worse every day.

She haunted him in his dreams, on his dates, when he sat at the typewriter and tried to write. He even found her—and her children!—hovering at his elbow when he tried to do a little Christmas shopping.

"A wise choice," the salesgirl said when he picked up a backpack to study the construction. Those are our bestselling children's models." He'd thrown it down in disgust and left the store.

Maybe I should leave the country, he thought then. *Take on a really challenging story to get my juices flowing again. Something that wouldn't leave any time or energy to think about women.*

He sprang up from his chair and strode to the closet for a coat. His editor, Neil Baxter, would find him a story, or else. Because Neil Baxter was the one who had made the reservations at the Talbot's Family Resort. Because, he decided, if it hadn't been for Neil Baxter he wouldn't be in this mess in the first place.

"You owe me one, old buddy," he said, stabbing the elevator button that would take him to the ground floor of his apartment building.

The day outside was clear and cold with a wind blowing in off the bay that sliced right through to your bones. Grant breathed deeply, savoring the fresh ocean smell without really being aware of it. He was unaware, too, of the Christmas lights and ornaments that decorated both sides of the street.

Grant Saxon was hardly in a holiday mood.

Neil's secretary was a new one. At least, Grant amended mentally, she hadn't been sitting behind the desk the last time he'd dropped by Neil's office. She was a redhead, of course—one of the curvy kind that Neil had a particular fondness for, with a glimmering cascade of hair and a mouth that was made to sell lipstick. Grant was a little alarmed to realize that she didn't raise his temperature even a tenth of a degree.

"Please go right in, Mr. Saxon," she said, smiling at him as she replaced the intercom with which she had alerted Neil to his presence. "Mr. Baxter will be happy to see you."

"I want an overseas assignment," Grant said without preamble. "Preferably yesterday."

Neil looked up from the papers he was reading. He had coal-black hair, dark blue eyes and teeth so white that when he smiled you were in danger of being blinded. He smiled. "When am I going to get the rest of this?"

Grant ignored the question, flinging himself into a chair in front of Neil's desk. "I heard rumors to the effect that *National Geographic* is putting together a team to do a piece on the caravans of North Africa. I want to be on it."

"When am I going to get the rest of this?" Neil said again.

Grant scowled. "The rest of what?"

"This." He held up the first page of a book manuscript. It had Grant's name on it.

Grant shrugged. "When I get the time," he said, dismissing it. "I heard that Pete Jackson has already been assigned to do the pictures."

"Make time."

"He's probably the— What?"

"Make time. The faster you get it finished, the faster we can get it published."

"Just like that?"

"Just like that. This is some of the best stuff you've ever done. If the rest of it reads like this, I can practically guarantee you a movie out of it."

"Just like that?" Grant said again.

"Just like that. How soon can I have it?"

Grant hesitated. How soon could he have it? "How the hell do I know how soon you can have it?" he said irritably. Those two chapters had been written in cabin four of Talbot's Family Resort when he was supposed to be working on an article about the recreational wonders of Bend, Oregon. But he hadn't written one word since he'd been back in San Francisco. Not one word. On anything.

"Is there a problem, Grant, ol' buddy?"

"Damn right there's a problem!"

"And?"

"You made those reservations up in Oregon, didn't you?"

"Yes." Neil began to smile, half knowing what was coming.

"At the Talbot Family Resort?"

"Yes." The smile got wider.

"One Lily Talbot, proprietor?"

The smile became a full-fledged grin. "Toothsome little morsel, isn't she? You two hit it off?"

"Like gangbusters." Grant's scowl would have cowed a lesser man. Or one that knew him less well. "I think I'm in love with her, dammit!" he swore, saying it aloud for the first time. It wasn't quite as bad as he thought it would be. Not quite.

"And?"

"And what? It's ruined my writing, that's what! It's ruined my social life! Dammit to blazing hell, it's ruined my sex life!"

"And?"

"Why do you keep saying 'and'? And what? She's got three kids! You know that as well as I do. I'm not ready for that kind of responsibility," he said. "I'm not ready to get married, let alone try to be a father." A sudden thought struck him with the force of a thunderbolt, bringing him upright in his chair. "She could be pregnant," he said, remembering their last passionate encounter. She'd scrambled his brain so thoroughly that he'd forgotten all about protection.

Pregnant, he thought. And she'd never said a word. Knowing her, she wouldn't, either. She'd just go on and have the baby all by herself and never try to force him to live up to his responsibilities. Never considering for a moment that he might *want* to live up to them. He shot up out of his chair.

"I've got to go," he said, leaving Neil sitting there with his mouth hanging open.

HE ARRIVED at Talbot's Family Resort at eleven o'clock at night in the middle of a record snowfall on Christmas Eve. The No Vacancy sign was lit, its red glow complementing the strings of multicolored Christmas lights outlining the peaked roof and windows of the rambling old building. The porch light was burning as it had been the first time he'd ever seen the lodge, its golden glow a feeble beacon, glimpsed now through a curtain of snow.

He sat in the car for a long moment, wondering if she'd still be up, wondering if she'd be glad to see him, wondering if she'd even let him in.

Because the simple, inescapable truth was that he'd walked out on her. Never mind that she'd given him leave to do it. That she'd all but pushed him out the door. He'd walked out on a woman who just might possibly be carrying his child.

He hoped she was. Then he'd have to marry her.

"Quit acting like a feebleminded snake, Saxon," he said to himself. "Get out of the car."

The walk to her front door was the longest he had ever taken. His fist as he raised it to knock was as heavy as a mallet. And the time she took to answer was an eternity. But the look in her eyes when she opened the door was more than worth waiting for.

Lily heard the muffled knock through the soft strains of the Christmas carols playing on the stereo. *Who in the world?* she thought, not immediately moving toward the front door. *The middle of a snowstorm on Christmas Eve and I get visitors!*

"And no room at the inn," she said, smiling at her own wit.

The knock came again.

Lily set her hot chocolate down on the coffee table and went toward the door. She stopped less than an arm's length away from it, staring at the hulking shadow on the other side. There was something familiar about the figure silhouetted in the windowed upper half of the door. Something achingly, heart-stoppingly familiar.

Grant. Grant Saxon was at her front door.

Oh, Lord!

She reached out hurriedly and yanked it open. "Grant." Her voice was serene and surprised, joyous and frightened all at once. She had known he would come back. One day. But not nearly so soon. She had hoped he would come back to stay. But really didn't believe he would. "Come in. Please, come in," she said breathlessly, stepping back to invite him inside. "It's freezing out there."

He laughed nervously. "I think this is where I came in the last time."

Her soft laugh echoed his. "Yes, I think it is. Well, never mind. Come in, anyway." She closed the door behind him and turned away, leading the way to the living room.

Grant stopped in the open archway, a feeling of utter peace and belonging settling over him like a warm, fleecy blanket. *Home*, he thought, taking in the welcoming scene that greeted him. This was home, dressed up for Christmas. Done as only Lily could do it.

A Yule log burned in the stone fireplace. Hand-knit stockings hung from the mantel, each labeled with a child's name. Evergreen boughs and holly berries decorated the tops of doors and the mantelpiece and made a fragrant backdrop for the Nativity scene on the sideboard against the far wall. Bayberry candles and beribboned baskets of pinecones scented the air. A Christmas tree, nearly seven feet tall and hung with popcorn and cranberries and one-of-a-kind ornaments, held pride of place in front of the bookcase.

And in the middle of it all stood Lily, in her blue chenille robe with her hair pulled back in a ponytail and a tiny smudge of whipped cream on the end of her nose, looking like the angel come down from the top of the tree.

Saxon, you jackass, you must have been crazy to leave, even for just one measly, miserable minute.

"I was just filling the stockings," Lily said, smiling a little self-consciously when he just stood there staring at her. "You know, walnuts and oranges and candy canes and little Matchbox cars. I was, um, having a little hot chocolate. With just a drop of brandy. Would you like a cup? There's cranberry bread, too, if you're hungry." She began to move toward the kitchen. "Or how about an omelet? I think I have some mushrooms."

"You have whipped cream on your nose."

She flushed and reached up quickly to wipe it off but found her wrist caught in his hand. "Allow me. Please."

He leaned forward slowly, his eyes holding hers, giving her plenty of time to evade him, and delicately licked the tip of her nose. "Delicious," he said softly.

She stared up at him, her eyes huge and soft and blue and wanting. "Grant?"

"I love you, Lily," he said, and took her in his arms.

She melted into his embrace as if it had been only minutes instead of nearly a month since the last time he had held her. Her lips opened under his, acquiescing to the fevered demands of his tongue as naturally as if she did it every day of her life. Her whole heart and mind and body responded as if there had never been any doubt or indecision or hesitation.

"I love you, Lily," he said again, his lips ravishing her chin and cheeks and the tender skin at her temples. "I love you." His lips touched her ear. "That's the first time I've ever said that to a woman," he murmured against her closed eyes. "The first time I ever wanted to say it." Then, "No, no, that's not true. I wanted to say it the last time we made love."

He cupped her face in his hands and looked down at her, his brown eyes glowing with all the love in his heart. "That last time in the tent when you said you loved me— I wanted to say it then but something held me back. Habit, maybe, or my own stupidity. I thought if I didn't actually say it, if I didn't admit what I was beginning to feel, that it couldn't really be happening. If I didn't admit that you were becoming important to me, then you wouldn't be." The words tumbled out in a torrent, as if he had saved them all up and had to say them now, before some magical time limit was reached.

"But then the kids started being important to me, too. It happened with Lizzie first. Who could help loving Lizzie? And then realizing that, somehow, for some reason, Jeff had decided to accept me. I didn't think it mattered—his antagonism—but it did. And I was glad when it was gone. And finding Sean that morning. The relief was so great... Too great. So I ran, thinking 'Out of sight, out of mind,' but it didn't work that way. You were always there with me, Lily. You and the kids. Lizzie and Sean and Jeff. All of you tangled up in my heartstrings so that I didn't know where I left off and you began."

"Oh, Grant, darling," she whispered tenderly, her eyes shimmering with happiness and love. "I love you, too. So much. So very much. I nearly died when you left. And yet... and yet I love you so much that I couldn't make you stay if you didn't want to, even if I'd known how."

He kissed her again, bending slightly to lift her in his arms so that he could carry her to the sofa. He sat down with her in his lap, kissing her lips and her face and the soft wedge of skin just above the eyelet ruffle on her nightgown before drawing back to smile at her. "I have something for you," he said softly.

She pressed her lips to his throat. "Something more than this?"

He reached into his inside pocket and pulled out a small square box. "Merry Christmas, Lily."

It fitted her perfectly, a classic diamond solitaire that slid smoothly onto the third finger of her left hand. He kissed it in place and then kissed away her joyful tears, sliding his hand inside the folds of her robe.

"The last time we made love we didn't use anything," he said, his palm caressing her abdomen. "Is it too early to tell if I'm going to be the father of your next child?"

"Do you want to be?"

"Yes." There was utter conviction in his voice. "Yes, I want to be. Am I?"

"Not this time," Lily whispered, regret making her voice husky. How she'd love to be carrying Grant's child! "But we can try again," she said. "As many times as it takes. I— Oh, Grant!" She moaned softly as his hand slipped down her belly to cover the yearning warmth between her thighs.

"Now?" he said eagerly, caressing her gently through the cloth of her nightgown. "Can we make a baby now?"

For the first time in her life Lily didn't think of her children or what was proper or anything else but the man who was caressing her so tenderly. Instead, she gently disengaged herself from his arms and stood up.

"Yes, let's make a baby now," she said, taking his hand to lead him to her bedroom.

There was the remnant of a fire burning on the hearth in the room, its dying embers casting a faint, rosy glow over the homey quilted coverlet on her bed. Without letting go of his hand, she drew the quilt back and then the blankets, exposing the pale blue sheets with their flower-trimmed borders. She reached for the belt on her robe and tugged it open.

"Allow me," Grant said softly, brushing her hand out of the way. He smiled a secret lover's smile. "Please."

Lily dropped her hands to her sides.

"I've been dreaming of undressing you every night for a month now," he told her, pushing the robe off her shoulders. It fell in a heap around her feet. Grant sighed. "I knew your nightgown would look like this," he said, running a fingertip over the eyelet trim that decorated the bodice of her gown and the hems of the tiny cap sleeves.

"Like what?"

He nudged one sleeve downward, his palm caressing the silky skin of her shoulder. "Sweet and sexy," he sighed, bending to kiss her.

Lily stretched her neck sideways, offering him more. Offering him everything. He kissed the rounded part of her shoulder, moving slowly up the side of her neck to her ear, along her jaw, her cheeks, her closed eyelids, her nose and, finally, her lips. Lily melted against him, boneless and pliant, yet strong as a passionate woman is strong.

Her mouth opened, avid and seeking; her arms circled his waist, pulling him to her; her thighs pressed against his. She moaned deep in her throat, the sound both an invitation and a demand. Her hips rotated against his, echoing the sentiment. And then her hands began tugging at the fabric of his shirt, pulling it from the waistband of his jeans. For the first time in her life, Lily found herself taking the initiative in lovemaking.

It felt wonderful.

"Hurry," she murmured, dragging her mouth from his. "Oh, please, hurry. I want to touch you. I *need* to touch you." She took a step backward, her soft blue eyes blazing up into his with the fierce, hot passion of a woman aroused and in love. "I need you to touch me," she breathed, reaching up to pull her nightgown from her shoulders.

The elastic neckline let it slide off her body easily, ending up in a heap on top of the already discarded robe. She stepped out of it. Then, naked, she reached for the buttons on Grant's shirt.

"Hurry," she said again, trying to slip them from their buttonholes. Her hands were clumsy, trembling with a passion she didn't even try to contain.

Grant gasped and reached up with both hands. Buttons flew everywhere. And Lily, quintessential mother, homemaker extraordinaire, didn't even notice. She helped him tear it open.

A minute later, he was as naked as she was. Together they fell onto the bed, kissing and caressing and whispering words of undying love and passion. Apologies for hurts both imagined and real. Regrets for time wasted. Promises for the future—all of the words finally blending into the sighs and murmurs and moans of lovers everywhere as his body slid into hers. Cul-

mination came quickly; a grand, glorious, intoxicating release of emotion that left them both gasping for
breath when it was over.

"I've died and gone to heaven," Grant said when he
had the breath to speak.

"No." Lily shook her head against the pillows, her
eyes shining up into his. She touched his cheek gently,
cupping it in the palm of her hand. "You've come
home."

Epilogue

Christmas Eve, one year later.

"HOW'S THE EDITING COMING?" Grant asked, setting his wife's traditional cup of Christmas Eve chocolate, sans brandy, on the coffee table in front of her.

"Almost done." She put the computer-printed manuscript to one side and smiled up at her husband. "It's really terrific," she said. "Neil will be ecstatic."

"But will it sell?"

"Of course it will sell," she said indignantly, not allowing even Grant to malign Grant's work. She patted the sofa. "You do realize, don't you," she said, cuddling up to him as he settled down next to her, "that this will be our only Christmas absolutely alone?"

"How do you figure that?" He patted the eight month swell of her belly approvingly. "Looks to me like we have plenty of company."

She gave him a wry look. "You know what I mean. The kids are at their father's this year and the twins aren't due until January 18. I hope," she added, glancing down at the huge, ungainly mound that had taken over her lap. "Next year we'll have all five of them here, and then the year after that just Mutt 'n' Jeff here, and so on and so forth."

"Till death do us part," Grant added, entwining her fingers with his.

"No regrets?"

"Not a single one."

"You don't miss the bachelor life even a little bit? Exploring unknown territory?" she prodded him. "Risking your neck for a story? All that excitement?"

"Fishing for compliments?"

"Yes, please. I'm feeling fat."

He grinned, his brown eyes sparkling at her over his cup of chocolate. "You *are* fat."

She stuck her bottom lip out at him. "That's not a nice thing to say to a pregnant lady."

"Beautifully fat," he amended, lifting her hand to his lips. "Gloriously round. Spectacularly rotund." He looked at her over their clasped hands. "Enough?" he said.

"Enough."

"Then, to answer your question. No, I don't miss the bachelor life even one tiny bit. I get all the excitement I can stand, and then some, every time we make love. And this—" he touched her belly with the back of his hand, keeping their fingers entwined "—and the other three kids are still a bit of unknown territory to me. As long as I have them and you, I don't need anything else."

Mills & Boon

YOU'RE INVITED TO ACCEPT
4 TEMPTATIONS
AND A
DIGITAL QUARTZ
CLOCK
FREE!

Acceptance card

This month's
irresistible novels from

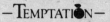

—TEMPTATION—

WIT AND WISDOM by Shirley Larson

What was Joel Brandon doing at the kids' summer camp
where Alison was teaching? He had finished their
relationship – so why was he pursuing her now?

HERO IN DISGUISE by Gina Wilkins

Settling down was not for Summer Reed. Party by night,
work by day and let tomorrow take care of itself – that
was her motto. But when Derek Anderson crashed into
her life, Summer was dismayed to find he had other plans
for her future.

A WANTED MAN by Regan Forest

What with all the cattle rustling going on, brand
inspector Beth Connor was suspicious of everyone.
Especially a certain skinny-dipping drifter she caught
red-handed with two of her neighbour's horses.

TEMPTING FATE by JoAnn Ross
(Final novel in this delightful trilogy)

Gorgeous, sexy Brooke had been Donovan Kincaid's
college sweetheart, and now the two of them were
reunited – but on a professional level only. Donovan was
determined to change that . . .

Spoil yourself next month
with these four novels from

— TEMPTATION —

THIS THING CALLED LOVE
by Marion Smith Collins

Samantha Hyatt thought she had all the answers when
it came to romance. After all, she had written a book on
the subject, hadn't she? And love at first sight was not
to be trusted! But her theories fell apart when she met
irresistible Max Stanwood who urged her to join him in
a headlong plunge into love.

BEFORE AND AFTER by Mary Jo Territo

Verna Myers found the courage to change her image, and
a spa seemed just the best place to start. Mel Hopkins fell
in love with Verna instantly. But though the feeling was
mutual, each thought the other couldn't see past the
flaws to the sexy person inside.

HONOURABLE INTENTIONS
by Judith McWilliams

Jenny Ryton was perfectly happy living over her quilt
shop with a nine-year-old genius. But when a Social
Services caseworker told her she would lose her young
charge because she was single, Jenny vowed to marry.
There was only one problem – finding a willing groom.

ON THE WILD SIDE by Kate Jenkins

What did he, A. Barclay Carstairs, up-and-coming
lawyer and responsible citizen, want with a zany, playful
sprite like Silky Phelan, a rock DJ? But Silky had
insinuated herself into his every thought and he knew his
careful plans were in danger.